But the Angels Never Came

Eric James-Olson

DEDICATION

To Amelia, Holly, Sean, and Dr. Mikey

CONTENTS

NOTE FROM THE AUTHOR

It is with pleasure that I present to you the prequel to *Farmers and Cannibals.*

In writing *But the Angels Never Came,* I was influenced by several classic texts. Genesis, the books that pertain to Abram, was the main source from which the plot and characters were derived. Other sources of inspiration included the following: Leviathan, The Old Regime and the Revolution, The Prince, The Antichrist, Beyond Good and Evil, The Dialogues of Plato, and Objectivist philosophy.

With this said, I would like to add that my goal in writing *But the Angels Never Came* was not to push some moral or philosophical agenda.

I hope you enjoy reading it, as much as I enjoyed writing it!

CHAPTER I

"Have you heard the story of Abraham?" The oldest man in the group asked as his companions stared into the remains of the fire. There were only four of them there. The women had gone to sleep and only one of the children was still awake.

The child had heard the story once before, but that was a long time ago from a different storyteller. That storyteller and all the other men and women of that group were ambushed and slaughtered. The child had somehow survived.

The men were not really listening, thinking instead of the long trek that awaited them at sunrise.

"Tell it again," the child begged, "I have heard it once before, but never from you."

"Well, if you haven't heard it from me, you haven't heard it at all," the old man said and began the telling of this well-known and often repeated tale.

In the old nation there were laws for everything. It was a much more complicated world, and it required very complicated laws. The laws were many, and there were people who spent their lives learning them. Before the world ended, Abraham was one of these people.

When the insurgents came, Abraham was a very young man. But he already had a family. A wife named Sarah, and a young teenage boy they called Iniko. Now, Iniko did not come easy. He did not come the natural way. Sarah was barren, but in the old nation the people had a way of taking the seed from one woman, and planting it in another. A friend of Sarah's, Haley was her name, agreed to carry the child and to deliver him into the world.

On the day of his birth, Abraham and Sarah were euphoric. All the years of trying to have a baby, all the years of hoping that it would happen, all the nights spent wondering if it would ever be possible were finally over. The couple was overjoyed to finally be a happy family.

The final year of the world 2066, before the beginning of the moon calendar, Abraham was living in the city. The city that Abraham lived in had been at the center of all industry, production, and business. Before the occupation this was a city with millions of people and buildings as tall as the mountains. The people ruled themselves; the people looked as if they came from all different parts of the world, yet; they all spoke one language; they all lived together under the same rules, the same laws.

You see, there was a great famine throughout the entire world. There were so many people and there just wasn't enough food for everybody to live on. Well, at least that is what we were all told. Naturally, our people have become suspicious of a real reason aside from what we were told.

Land on which to grow food became more precious than life, and the great nations of the world banded together to ensure that resources would be used for their own.

Sometimes, when a smaller nation refused to join the alliance, the great nations would force the smaller to pay in resources. The smaller kept its right to rule, and the bigger got what it wanted. Other times, especially if the leaders of the great nations thought that the land could be used more productively, meaning that the people weren't making enough food, instead of forcing a payment; they forced the people off the land.

In these cases, robotic men and murderous flying machines were sent. The people in the cities, those living in the suburbs, those in the country were killed en masse.

In 2064, The Great Alliance formed out of the three Super-States: The Eurasians, the United-Americans, and The Democratic Republic of the Pacific, was willing to give our old nation a chance at retaining its sovereignty. The cost was great. Farms were nationalized. Politicians could be heard every day and every night.

The quota was not reached. In fact, the reports claimed that productivity was cut in half. A great food shortage followed. Many people starved. We all wondered, "How could this be?" After all, most of the farms were fully mechanized. There was nothing that could be done to make the machines more efficient and that year we had more rain than any year that I can remember. Maybe we were lied to. Maybe we were set up. But what difference does it make now? Now we will never know.

The official occupation began in 2065. The leaders of the old nation let it happen. After the nationalized farms failed, the leaders still refused to join the alliance. Submission was all that was asked. The rest of the world was already conquered or enfolded into the protective embrace of a Super-State.

Allied forces occupied the cities and the countryside.

At first, the occupying soldiers were not much of a bother, but during the first month there were several terrorist attacks. The terrorists were called insurgents. That is what they called our people when we defended ourselves.

Soldiers were killed, their replacements retaliated. Martial law was decreed throughout the cities. Identification checks, curfews, arrests without warrant, and executions without trials, started a vicious cycle with one certain outcome.

In the months leading up to The Cleansing, there were terrorist attacks every day. The terrorists bombed and shot at soldiers, sympathizers, business owners, and the leaders of the old nation that refused to give up power. Assassinations were commonplace but no-one felt badly for the power hungry politicians.

It was the collateral damage that fueled the cycle. The allies were able to show the people of their nations that we were lawless savages and nothing else. The use of force was then justified. More force was used and the terrorists felt justified in seeking revenge. I can't help but wonder: was this the plan all along? Did the leaders of the allied powers intend for this? Was it inevitable for the occupation to lead to the rightful, at least in the eyes of the rest of the world, annihilation of an entire nation?

Well, anyway I digress; you probably didn't understand any of that did you. You're just a boy and this is the only world you have ever lived in. Let me get back to Abraham.

Abraham had known that something terrible was going to happen. I suppose that most of the men and women his age, who fled to the mountains and survived, must have known something wasn't right when the occupiers ordered all citizens to report immediately to their local registration centers. Within twelve hours every man, woman, and child was expected to report.

News bulletins popped up on screens throughout every corner of the old nation. I can still remember the message, "Acts of terror can no longer be controlled. For your own safety, report to your nearest registration center. Anyone found elsewhere after six p.m. will be executed."

Abraham was in the city when he saw the bulletin. He was actually within sight of his registration building. For several minutes he stood in front of the large impermanent structure. It's hard to say exactly what he must have been thinking, standing at a crossroads. A step in one direction and he would have faded away into history as a nameless face. A step in the opposite direction and, well, that is why his story is told. He took a step in the opposite direction.

Strangely enough, I heard that it was a crack in the foundation of the hastily constructed building that caused Abraham to turn around, to disobey the order that threatened certain death to noncompliants. The crack, which would have seemed insignificant to any other citizen of the old nation, told Abraham quite clearly: stay away, something isn't right here.

He listened to the warning and walked directly home. He passed several of his friends and neighbors walking in the opposite direction. An old friend asked with a puzzled look on his face, "Abraham, where you going?"

Abraham didn't answer. He continued to look straight ahead as if the old friend was a stranger.

He arrived home to find that his wife was still at work. It occurred to Abraham immediately that he made a mistake. He should have called her right away. She may have already left for the registration center. With a look of intense fear in his eyes he commanded his phone to call his wife. He paced nervously hoping desperately that she would pick up the call, praying that she was still at work.

"Hello darling," she said casually, as Abraham took a deep breath. Without noticing, he had stopped breathing when he first realized his mistake.

Abraham couldn't contain his elation at hearing her voice. "Sarah, I thought for sure that you'd be at the registration center."

When she responded the casual tone was gone. She said, "Well, I was just about to leave the office. I heard that we are all to report immediately." She paused for a moment and said, "Are you ok?" with deep concern.

"Yes, I'm ok," he said. "I just. I just don't think we should report. Something's wrong. Why would they have us all report? It has never happened before. And why would we have to all report by a certain time? Why do they want us to all be there at six?"

"I don't know," she said, "But I do know the alternative. They'll kill us if we don't go. What's the worst that could happen?"

"I don't want to find out," he said. "I have an idea. The three of us. We can't tell this to anyone. The three of us will take the car. We'll drive out of town."

"But what about the checkpoints?" Sarah interjected, "They are sure to stop us at the checkpoints. Abraham, this is not like you. "

His answer to that was a simple negation, "We'll worry about it when we get there. Anyway, we'll drive out of town, into the mountains. We can go to that old hotel that we stayed at once. Remember for our first anniversary. That one on top of the mountain. I can't remember what that was called."

"Church Peak.," she answered, "that was a beautiful weekend."

"Yea," he said, "that's the one. It's been abandoned now

for almost a year, since the occupiers first came. We'll go up to Church Peak and wait this whole thing out. If it turns out that there was nothing to worry about, we'll just say that we left for an evening in the country and our car broke down. If there really is something to worry about, we'll just stay up there as long as we need to."

After a minute of silence Sarah said "I can't believe I'm saying this, but I think you're right. I think we should do it. What about Iniko? We have to get him from school."

"I'm already walking out the door," he said, "Just get yourself home and I'll meet you in an hour."

Abraham ended the call before his wife could respond. "I trust you," she said, but he did not hear.

Haran Middle School was only a mile away. Before departing for the school Abraham looked out on the city. The brilliant skyscrapers were awe inspiring under the morning sun. In the center, The African-Communications corporate office towered over the rest. The building had stood as a testament to all the progress made in the last quarter century by the people of the old nation. It still stood that fateful day when Abraham decided to leave the city, yet it had lost all meaning. A hollow memorial was all that remained of the once industrious hub. The business left, the employees were scattered about.

Abraham turned his gaze away from the skyline and got in his car. Haran Middle School was only a mile away. Abraham parked in the school lot and walked up to the entrance.

He read the message posted on a large screen at the front of the building: All students will report to the registration center immediately after lunch. He walked inside. The secretary seemed busy. He walked past the main office to his son's English class. Without saying a word he grabbed his son's arm. The instructional robot at the front of the room was not trained for this type of circumstance. As it repeated, "Good afternoon, welcome to Eighth Grade English. How can I help you sir?" Abraham left the classroom with his son.

When the father and son reached the car, Abraham got in first. It wasn't until the moment when Iniko shut the car door that Abraham began to explain. "We are going to pick up your mother and we're driving out to the mountains. Although Iniko was a naturally inquisitive boy, he was also an obedient son, obedience learned from his father. No other explanation was necessary.

Sarah prepared several bags for the journey. Food, water, and clothing were the main supplies. She also packed hiking and camping equipment. When Abraham walked in the door, he nearly tripped over a bag full of meal bars. Regaining his balance he called his wife's name, "Sarah," he said, "Iniko was still at school, he's in the car now."

Sarah walked out of the bathroom. In her hand, she was holding an ancient revolver, a gun that she had inherited as an heirloom. Years ago, she took Iniko out to the county to fire the old gun. Purely for sport, purely for the exhilaration of firing such an antiquated piece of machinery, Sarah and Iniko drove out to her grandfather's old farm when the weather was nice. On an old fence, Sarah placed targets. Old bottles and cans left by squatters were placed on the fence and then shot off.

During the first week of the occupation, when the insurgents ordered residents to turn in all firearms, Sarah hid the gun and three boxes of bullets in a hole that she had cut in the drywall behind the bathroom mirror.

When Abraham saw his wife with the gun he asked, "You still have that thing?" and said, "clever lady."

"Not that clever," she said, "I just couldn't see myself parting with it."

Abraham smiled. He watched as his wife packed the gun and the boxes of bullets. It took the couple two trips to bring the baggage down the four flights of stairs out the back entrance of their apartment building where the car was parked. Abraham supposed that neither the stairs nor the back door had cameras. In contrast, the front door had several, and during the day, two soldiers posted at the entrance.

Once in the car, Abraham put an arm around his son. Sarah logged onto the car's computer and entered the coordinates for the bridge leading out of town. She turned her head in the direction of her husband. She forced a smile, and Abraham blinked, maintaining a steady and serious countenance. The nervous tension felt by Abraham and Sarah was immense. Iniko must have known something was wrong, but he never said a word.

The driverless car drove through the city at a regular pace

minding the expected speed for all vehicles. Abraham's family traveled in silence all the way to the bridge knowing that there might be soldiers posted. The bridge was a checkpoint.

In the year leading up to Abraham's famous sojourn out of the city, whenever there was a serious terrorist attack, or any reason for a temporary heightening of security, all cars were stopped and checked at the bridge. Sometimes cars were turned around. Other times cars were let through. In some cases the cars were stopped and the passengers were asked to pull over. In these cases the car was impounded and the passengers were typically shot.

During the ride out of the city, even Iniko knew that the bridge was a potential danger. At school the children told stories; he heard rumors from his friends and didn't have any reason to think these rumors false. Almost once a week, Iniko was told a tale of one of his friend's parents. Although it was never one of his friends, it always seemed to be a friend of friend, a kid that everyone knew, but a kid that no-one actually knew. Usually it was the father of the family who drove out to the bridge. In the stories the father never came back. The kids would joke and snicker that the father was a terrorist, a traitor, an agitator, all the words that the children heard on the news, the words that their parents used with bitter sarcasm during their quiet conversations late at night when they thought their children were in bed.

A mile from the bridge Iniko began to quiver noticeably. Abraham tried to calm his son by running his hand through his hair, but he stopped after a moment. His hand was shaking too. Abraham realized that he had no plan for the inevitable likelihood of meeting armed soldiers at the bridge. Several ideas attacked his understanding at once. He could play dumb. He could turn around at the last minute. He could drive straight through the checkpoint without stopping.

Sarah pulled out the gun and loaded it.

Sarah said to Abraham, "I've never seen more than three posted guards at the bridge. Everyone's so scared of the bridge that they don't actually need that many soldiers. When they pull us over, I'll get out and play dumb. That's what everyone does, so they won't expect anything out of the usual. When their backs are turned, shoot them in the back of the head."

There were only two guards. As the car pulled up, the first guard, a largely built woman with dark skin and a big smile asked Abraham to pull over the car. She used the tip of her rail gun to point toward a spot on the side of the road. In addition to her intimidating fire arm, a weapon that could cut a man in half with a single projectile, she wore full body armor. The armor covered her head leaving only a small space where a bullet could penetrate her neck. Her face was also unprotected, but Abraham was afraid to pull the revolver out while she faced him. He assumed that she would draw her weapon faster than him.

Abraham and Sarah were still in the car when the guard asked, "Did you know that everyone is to report to the registration centers?"

Abraham mumbled something incomprehensible and then said, "No, we haven't heard. We were planning on taking a short trip out to the country."

"Shouldn't your boy be in school?" the guard asked, her eyes sharpening.

"Well, yes" Abraham said. Before he could continue his explanation the guard asked him to get out of the car.

Abraham felt the weight of the revolver in his jacket pocket. He shifted the gun and released the safety. He squeezed the grip and put his finger on the trigger. Suddenly, as if on cue, Sarah jumped out of the car. She took a few steps past the guard, enough that the guard had to turn her back on the car. The guard pointed her rail gun at Sarah and screamed, "Get on the ground!"

Sarah said, "Oh, I'm sorry, I thought you wanted me to get out of the car.

The guard screamed again. "Get on the ground you dumb bitch."

Abraham was already out of the car. In a movement he placed the barrel of the gun on the guard's neck. Before he could fire she turned around. Her face was uncovered. Abraham fired the revolver into her left eye socket.

As the guard fell, Sarah caught her rail gun. She pointed the weapon at the second guard. The projectile went through the body armor covering his chest, through his torso, and through the other side of his body armor.

Sarah stood up. Her eyes wandered over to her husband mysteriously. An ambiguous grin was hidden under her lips. The deed was terrible, but she enjoyed the sensation. It wasn't murder. Sarah abhorred the idea of murder. To kill with no reason, to kill for individual profit with no respect to the rights of a fellow man was a concept so base, so terrible that she would have shuttered uncontrollably at just the thought. No, the deaths of these two guards were justified. As soldiers employed in the oppression of a people residing in a nation that should be sovereign, and as soldiers who were directly responsible for the unjust murder of innocent men, women, and children; they had given up their rights.

Abraham did not feel the same pleasure as his wife. His forehead was creased, his eyes downcast, and a heavy frown overwhelmed his face. He felt great sympathy for these victims of circumstance, yet he felt great relief as well.

Gradually, by degrees, he began to feel a strange sense of happiness. He was glad to be alive, but most of all, he was glad that he no longer had to worry about the uncertainty of the bridge. With the exception of an occurrence of some unlucky circumstance, the rest of the ride out to the mountains promised to be smooth; it promised to be without incident.

Abraham snapped out of his reverie and realized suddenly that Iniko was still in the car. Sarah noticed in the same moment. Iniko's eyes were wide. He was horrified. Abraham darted for the vehicle while Sarah pried the rail gun away from the dead soldier. She put the weapon in the trunk of the car as her husband comforted their son.

Once in the vehicle, Sarah programmed the car's computer to take the family to the hotel on top of Church Peak. The hotel wasn't just in the mountains; it was on top of a mountain. It was remote and according to her calculations, most likely abandoned. She did not make the same assumption as Abraham. She knew the possibility that others might have the same idea. Other families may have escaped to the mountains as well. Just because the hotel was out of business, did not necessarily mean that it was abandoned.

According to the calculations made by the car's computer, the ride out to the hotel would take just over four hours, about two-hundred miles. Abraham held his son tightly for the first three hours of the ride. Iniko fell asleep and Abraham allowed himself to relax.

"Boy it's sure getting late." The old storyteller noticed that the two men who had been sitting across from him had gone to sleep. The child was still listening intently.

"You can't stop now. You're about to get to the best part. How do you know so much about what happened? The other storytellers didn't know anything compared to you."

"I can see it all as if I were there. You know, I spent the best years of my life alongside Abraham. It was years ago when he united the twelve tribes. That was a great time, a time of peace, a time when you could trust your fellow man. We camped as one tribe under one name. Now, many of the

people have fallen back into darkness, back into cannibalism. Now the tribes reunite but once a year. Our people are spread far and wide. I suppose you know that though, you know that all too well. Anyway, when I met Abraham, it was about twenty years ago. He told me the entire story himself. He told it to me differently though. He told it in pieces, in reminiscences. During the years that I knew him I put the pieces together. When we parted I began telling it as one story. I've been telling it ever since."

The boy could not see the deceptive flicker in the eyes of the old storyteller as he spoke. "Then why can't you continue," the boy said, "I'm not tired."

"Oh, but I am, and we have a long walk ahead of us tomorrow. You know how important it is to stay on the move in these parts. Besides, we have almost two weeks before we reach the meeting place, and all told, I'll be lucky to get through the whole tale before the week is out."

CHAPTER II

The day's journey had been long and monotonous. These were the types of days the men prayed for. Boredom was always preferred over excitement, over an ambush. When the evening's chores were finally finished, when the women and most of the children had gone to sleep, and there were only four of the travelers left awake sitting around the fire, the old man resumed his tale. The boy listened with great attention.

When Abraham saw the cars blocking the road, he panicked. He switched the car to manual and stopped the vehicle in its tracks. He asked Sarah, "Is this some sort of blockade?"

Sarah stared out into the distance for several minutes trying to comprehend all that was in front of their car. "No soldiers, if it's a blockade, at least there isn't anyone manning it. Maybe we can get around."

Abraham nodded gravely and drove the car up to the heap

of twisted metal.

"It's not a blockade at all," Sarah said, "not an intentional one at least. Just an accident."

"Well that's rare," Abraham said, "I've never heard of a computer driverless car getting into an accident. One of the drivers must have had the car in manual."

Abraham and Sarah got out of their car to examine the damage. There were four cars involved in the wreck. The road was completely blocked.

Abraham uttered weakly, "It's strange that four cars would even be on the road at the same time. Since the occupation, these roads are barely used."

"I can't make any sense of it," Sarah answered.

Three of the cars seemed to have been headed in the same direction that Abraham's family was going before they stopped. Abraham investigated the first car. It was silver, a model similar to his own car. There was a driver and two passengers. Their eyes wore expressions of terror. The driver's head was bent in a sickeningly unnatural angle. One of the passengers had a gaping wound in her chest. The other's head was smashed in. Abraham gagged. The putrid smell of the decomposing corpses was overwhelming. He did not investigate the other cars.

After Abraham calmed down, his wife asked, "Do you think we can get around?"

"I'll try."

Iniko was awake, sitting politely in the back of the car. Sarah took him by the hand and invited him to stand aside with her while her husband attempted to drive around the pileup. There was a narrow strip of shoulder and a steep ditch. Abraham attempted to drive on the narrow strip staying as close as possible to the cars involved in the wreck. Half way across Abraham could feel the two tires on the passenger side of the car lift up slightly. He tried to correct this by steering the wheel in the direction of the wreck, away from the ditch. It was the wrong move.

Sarah watched in terror as the car started to tip over. Iniko screamed, "Father!" The car tumbled down the ditch rolling twice. It came to rest right side up. From the angle in which she was standing, Sarah couldn't see her husband; she couldn't tell if he was alright.

Suddenly the driver side door popped open. Abraham stepped out smiling. "Well, that didn't work," he said.

"You could have killed yourself. I shouldn't have let you." She ran up to her husband. Abraham pulled his wife close.

"I'm alright." He said still smiling. The grave manner and all his fears were gone.

It was fortunate that the car landed in way that it did. Although it was un-drivable, two of the wheels had popped off; the baggage in the car was easily accessible.

"I guess we're walking," Abraham said in calm reserve, uncharacteristic of his former self. Iniko had apprehensions, but he only voiced positive enthusiasm. Sarah had prepared for the possibility and maintained her indifferent, peaceful manner. She began pulling out the hiking and camping equipment. She had packed three backpacks. Each pack was for long distance trekking. The family went hiking for two weeks every summer, so they had all the gear necessary for the weeklong walk that lay ahead.

With Iniko's help, she packed each bag with water, meal bars, changes of clothing, sleeping necessities, and miscellaneous camping supplies. In Abraham's bag, she packed a family size tent and a small camp stove. Using a strap she designed a small holster for the revolver. She assumed that Abraham would carry the larger and heavier rail gun.

Meanwhile, Abraham used the car's computer to make maps of the area. With this completed, he took out his old registration card. "Hey, Iniko, Sarah, let me have your registration cards." He was smiling brightly.

Abraham found some small sticks that were lying near his old car. Piling the sticks up, he made a structure that resembled a small altar. On top of the altar, he placed the cards. "Hey Sarah," he said, "bring me a torch from the camping gear." With the torch, by his own volition, he burned the cards. "Our names are gone; our identities gone. We are no-one; we are nothing; we are meaningless. But I'm happy. We belong to no-one; we exist for ourselves."

As Abraham said this, his wife and son looked on with quiet reserve. The husband, the father was someone else, someone greater than he was before. Neither Sarah, nor Iniko could have determined precisely what had changed, but they both knew the change was for the better, and that Abraham never seemed happier in his life; he never seemed so natural before.

The cards burned quickly. Abraham pulled the maps out of his pocket. After several minutes he said with spirit and humor, "About fifty eight miles to Church Peak." He carefully folded the maps, placing these carefully in his pocket. "On the bright side, most of the walk will be on this flat even road. It's just the last twelve miles or so that are going to be tough."

Iniko smiled at his father.

"Yep," Abraham said, "I think if we move at an even, steady pace we should be able to get there in four days. We have plenty of food. There should be places where we can find water along the way. And, I'd bet that the hotel still has stockpiles of canned food from when it was still operational. It was abandoned so suddenly that I doubt they emptied out the larders. If need be, we can live there the rest of our lives. Why would we go back to the city when we could live at a mountaintop resort? I hope they still have the tennis courts; I love to play tennis, but I never have time anymore."

Abraham continued to talk like this for the rest of the afternoon. His son had realized after watching his parents kill the soldiers at the bridge that his life would never be the same. He knew that he was never going back to his home. He understood that he would never see his friends again. His parents went to the bridge, and he went with them. His former companions would call him a traitor, a terrorist, but he would never hear it said.

That evening, Abraham camped underneath the stars with his family. Over two years had passed since he last did this. He built a large campfire; it was four feet wide and waist high. Sarah told stories, funny stories with cartoonish characters. Iniko laughed uncontrollably. That night the family stayed up late and enjoyed each other; eating, laughing, and singing in outright defiance of the world around them, in ignorance of the dangers surrounding them. It would be several years later before Abraham allowed the fire to grow so large, to take the risk of drawing unnecessary attention to himself.

The morning began normally. The family had breakfast, packed up camp, and started the day's walk. The walking was easy. The road was flat.

It was the flatness of the road that enabled Sarah to see the large group of men in the distance. Unfortunately, this allowed the men to see Sarah as well. The men were camped along the side of the highway. Two vehicles were parked on the shoulder. Before Sarah could alert Abraham to the men's presence, one of the men was pointing and shouting in their direction. To Sarah's surprise, Abraham did not panic.

"Abraham," Sarah replied desperately, "They just got in their cars!" She dropped her pack. "We have to run!"

Iniko dropped his pack and prepared himself to run. Abraham stood as still and unwavering as a rock. He said,

"No, we won't run and we won't fight. These men are deserters. The vehicles are stolen. I've heard rumors. I've heard that there've been entire units that disbanded from the Coalition Army. Rumors claim moral reasons. It must have been these men that created the road block, these men that blocked the road to make distance between themselves and their pursuers. They're running scared but make no mistake; they are dangerous. They caused the accident back there. They killed those men and women in those cars. Cowards are often dangerous."

"So we're just going to let them kill us? " Sarah asked wildly.

"No," Abraham replied, "Not if you do exactly as I tell you." Abraham said this and the vehicles were not far away. "Sarah" he said, "Your life is not in danger. When the men see you, they will not want you dead; they will want you alive; they will want you for your body. I will tell them that you are my sister. I will offer my services with a rail gun."

"What about Iniko? What will be his lot?" Sarah asked.

"He is your son and my nephew." Abraham said, "The men will not harm him. He presents no danger to them. But, if they think that I'm your husband, I am a dead man, so you must agree to tell the men that you're my sister. Tonight, tease the men into thinking that they all have a chance. Make them fight for you. They'll be gentlemen at first. They won't be that way for long though. I think we can rely on their sense of fair-play for at least one night. That is your part. I don't have enough time to tell you mine. Know this: if my plan doesn't work, you and Iniko may have to leave in the middle of the night. You may have to leave me behind. If you are awakened by any commotion at all, run for the hills.

Abraham stood in front of his wife and child as the two vehicles pulled up in front of them. He stood with his hands on his hips. In this position he was still well over six feet tall. He must have had light features, blond hair, and pure blue eyes. Although I never met him as a young man, I can deduce these features as the necessary precedent for the man I did know. When young, he must have been a good looking man, handsome and strong, for as an old man he still was.

The rail gun that was taken off of the soldier at the bridge was resting at his feet. He struck a pose that said; I could have shot at you, but I didn't see the point.

Four men piled out of the first truck. Three more hopped out of the second. They carried side arms and compact rail guns. One of the men was clearly the leader of the group. He stood in the center while his men carried themselves in a variety of brash and contrived postures.

Before the leader could speak, Abraham took a step forward calmly. "Good morning gentlemen."

The deserters looked at each other uneasily. The leader cleared both nostrils, cleared his throat and stared at Abraham. Gradually, by degrees his eyes became unfocused. He stared not at Abraham, but at a point in the distant horizon through both time and space, a point that existed long ago. Seeing through the man standing before him, the leader watched the scene play out; the actors were different, but the event was exactly the same.

The leader, a tall man with Egyptian features broke out of his trance and spoke in a deep, commanding voice, "What are you doing with that rail gun? What are you doing walking down this road?"

Abraham was not intimidated. "I could ask similar questions," he said in answer.

Several of the deserters pointed gun barrels in Abraham's direction. The leader held Abraham's gaze with indefatigable determination.

Paralyzed by fear, neither Sarah nor Iniko was able to move. The tension mounted on both sides. Trigger fingers became itchy; the hands supporting the guns became shaky. Abraham and his family were in just as much danger from an accidental gun shot, as they were from a shot intentionally aimed and fired.

The tension, built up to an extreme was suddenly and completely released. The sound that ended the tension was resonant, thunderous. From deep within his gut, booming abruptly, the leader of the deserters laughed. With eyes full of tears he finally said, "Relax, the man is unarmed." His men dropped their weapons to their sides as he turned his attention towards Sarah, "And who might you be?" he said with greedy eyes, and a mischievous smile.

Sarah relaxed. She said politely, "My name is Sarah. This

is my son Iniko. His father was executed, a traitor. I left the city with my brother, but our vehicle collided with another car. There must have been something wrong with the computer. I've heard of similar incidents..."

"But Sarah," the leader interjected, "Do you mean to say that this is your brother, not your husband. I don't see any family resemblance."

"Well, you shouldn't. We have different fathers. Neither of us takes after our mother."

The men looked at one another and grinned devilishly. Sarah was forced to hide the disgust she felt, hide her impulse to pull out the revolver and shoot each man in his crooked mouth.

The leader turned to look at the men standing on either side of him, exchanging grins, winking at one of the men. "Well, I must say for the whole company; it is a pleasure to be in the presence of such a beautiful woman."

Sarah was very beautiful. Her black hair was long, and it suited her. Her skin had a deep olive complexion. Her facial features were sharp, well defined. She stood tall but carried herself lightly. She was very thin, but in great physical condition. She was a picture of feminine beauty from an older age. If she were alive today, she would create great jealousy among the women of the tribe and attempted infidelity among the men.

The leader introduced himself formally. "I'm Captain Farrow, and these are my former brothers in arms. We deserted our unit several months ago. Constantly on the move, we have lived in these mountains ever since. We're killers. That was our chief occupation when we were still in the city. None of us could do it anymore. Now, we only kill if it suits our needs. Now, we kill for ourselves and no-one else."

Abraham turned around to look at Iniko. Shaking perpetually, his son looked horrified. He turned back to Captain Farrow and said, "Well met. Just like you and your men, we also kill when it suits us. There are two guards lying dead at the bridge out of town because they tried to prevent our escape. Like you, we are fugitives. We offer to you our services. We have a week's worth of food, and I've become an expert with this rail gun."

Farrow could not hide the devious expression on his face. "Yes," he said, "Those are just the services we would be interested in." His eyes wandered over to Sarah and he said, "My lady, what services will you offer?"

With a flirtatious smile she replied, "Well, I have many talents. It depends on what you and your soldiers are interested in."

The same booming laughter that broke the standoff escaped from Farrow once again. The other deserters joined him but with less enthusiasm. "Get in the truck," he said, "you're all one of us now."

The vehicles were operated manually. The men drove off road until they came upon an old access road. The road was in terrible condition. Clearly, it had not been used in a couple of years. Abraham was seated next to one of the deserters. The ex-soldier hadn't shaved for over a month. His eyes looked glazed over. He smelt homeless. After half-an-hour Abraham asked, "Where are we going anyway?"

"To the cave."

"Oh, I see. And where is this cave?"

"You see that mountain ahead. It's on the other side."

"I see. Why that specific cave?"

The deserter looked as if he was just asked to move the heavens and the earth. He sighed deeply and said, "Shit man, you ask a lot of questions."

"Now that I'm part of your band, I would like to be informed."

From the front of the truck Farrow said, "Just answer his questions Earl. You're no good for anything else anyway."

Earl sighed. "Alright. We found the cave just after we deserted. Farrow was driving the truck like a madman. He thought we might have been followed. It was getting dark out and we came upon this access road. We just followed it until we came upon the cave. We've camped there ever since."

"I see." Abraham said. "Did you have enough supplies?"

"No," Earl said, "Of course not. That's why we were camped along the highway this morning." As if rehearsing a speech Earl continued, "Every few days we camp along the highway waiting to ambush a car coming by. Most of the cars are filled with people escaping from the city. People no-one cares about. They always have food and supplies. We make them pull over. We take their food; we take their gear; we take their batteries. Farrow says we could live like this forever, with full bellies and a charged vehicle. There's only one thing miss…"

"Why don't you shut up back there," Farrow exclaimed, cutting him off. "I said to answer his questions not to talk us all to death. You're boring the man."

For Abraham, everything now made sense. The cars involved in the pile-up were ambushed. These men were more dangerous than he first thought. They might have been running scared initially, but that was no longer the case. They were in control of the surrounding area. They were willing to kill and pilfer to get what they wanted, and the only reason that Abraham and Iniko were still alive, was so the men might have a better chance at getting what they want from Sarah. He was right about one thing though. If he and his family were to survive, he would have to act that night.

Surrounding the cave there were tents and hammocks. In the center, there was a large fire ring constructed of fallen rocks. It was early in the afternoon when they arrived at the camp, yet the entire encampment was shaded. The thick foliage surrounding the cave created an ominous shadow. Not a single ray of sunlight penetrated the gloom of this wicked grove.

Upon entering the camp, the men deposited their weapons in the cave and immediately retired to the hammocks. Even in the shade, the heat sapped the energy out of anyone foolish enough to resist the urge of inactivity. Abraham, trying to fit in, whispered to Iniko, "Find a place to lie down. Relax as the men relax. Eat as the men eat. Act as these men act." Following his own advice, Abraham laid down as well.

When Abraham awoke, a fire had been lit in the center of the camp. The men were busy finding additional logs to add to the blaze. Sarah was seated next to Abraham. Iniko was helping the men.

Abraham said one thing only to Sarah, "Do as I told you, and we will survive the night. The men are sporting. They'll want the respect of winning you, rather than reputation for taking you."

Disgusted, not at her husband's request; but rather, at his discernment of the circumstance, and his understanding of these men's minds, she nodded her head solemnly and said, "Their nature will be their downfall. I do this knowing that you will punish them without compassion, without sympathy, like dogs gone rabid."

"It will be a pleasure," he said, "holding the fate of these men's lives within the tight grasp of my bare hands."

These men thought themselves above punishment, beyond reproach, outside the graspable range of justice. No god existed for these men. And because no god existed for

Abraham, he was compelled to exact his own reprimand for these fiends of mankind.

Sarah remained seated as Abraham joined the deserters in the gathering of firewood. Normally, Sarah would have helped as well, but with these men she was expected not to. She had a role to play.

Abraham slipped away unnoticed into the cave. Earlier he had seen one of the men take his bag and drop it at the cave's mouth. Abraham found the bag and reached into a side pocket. He knew exactly where to find the item that he was looking for. He had purchased this item at a yard sale outside of town years ago.

He was driving around with an old friend. The friend noticed the yard sale so they pulled over. Finding mostly junk, the friends almost left empty handed when the antique handle and worn leather sheath caught Abraham's eyes. It was incredibly strange. The butt of the handle was in the shape of an octagon. The handle was made of hard leather. It was remarkably heavy. Abraham remembered holding the sheath close to his eyes. He tried to read the description printed on the back. Only two words were legible: 'Survival' and '1976'. The rest had been worn off.

He pulled out the curved blade. It was nearly the length of his hand, from palm to fingertip. The tip of the blade was sharpened on both sides. In the handle guard there were two perfectly drilled holes. Abraham remembered wondering aloud, "What were these used for?"

Above the handle guard there were a series of deep slits in

the metal. He figured these out immediately. He pulled the knife out of the sheath and rested his thumb on the deep slits in the metal for a better, tighter grip. He turned to the man in charge of the yard sale and said, "how much?"

"Just take it," the man said.

Abraham proudly carried the extra weight of the heavy knife in his backpack ever since. He loved telling the story to fellow hikers. He enjoyed explaining how he found his prized possession, a knife that was almost a century old yet in great condition.

This was the item that he pulled out of his bag in the cave. Quickly he tucked the sheathed knife in his pocket and resumed the gathering of wood with the deserters. He made sure not to treat Iniko as his son. He spoke to him in the same manner that he used with everyone else.

The fire illuminated the entire grove. In front of the cave, it was brighter at night than it was during the day. The dancing flames brought out the character in each man's facial features. The pretense of rigid toughness forced upon the lines of the men's faces during the day had been given up entirely. Abraham's eyes shifted from man to man. 'Boys' he reasoned to himself, as his own eyes bored into the young men's thoughts. Each man was thinking one thought only: 'how will I make her mine.'

Farrow was sitting across the fire speaking with Iniko. Abraham watched as his son nodded politely, agreeing with everything the older man was saying. He stood up and moved across the fire to sit next to the leader of this band of deserters.

Farrow turned toward Abraham and began speaking immediately. He didn't skip a beat. It was as if he had been speaking to Abraham the entire time.

"Mr. Abraham," he said in his deep monotone, "I suppose you haven't heard about what's been happening in the city."

Abraham replied, "No, I wouldn't know," in a tone that suggested indifference.

"While you and the boys were gathering kindling, I was on the truck's computer. You wouldn't believe what's happening back there."

"After the past two years, I think I could believe anything."

"Oh," Farrow said amused, "but you won't believe this."

"You can try me if you like," Abraham said yawning into his hand.

"It's all over the news," Farrow said, "the people of your city. They've gone crazy. They're not just rioting. They're not just blowing up buildings or themselves. They're killing each other in the streets. I watched a video. An old woman was beating a young child mercilessly. It was the sickest thing I've ever seen."

Hiding his surprise, Abraham said with unnatural ease, "but why would the people of the city do that?"

As if he didn't hear Abraham's question, Farrow said, "The video, it shows some crazy shit. Three of the rioters…I don't know what else to call them, ran up to the man who was filming. They were babbling incomprehensibly. I couldn't make out a word they were saying."

Abraham stared into the fire for several minutes ruminating in silence. Farrow broke into his thoughts saying, "According to the official report, by allowing the city to fall into complete anarchy, the government has broken the peace treaty with The Great Alliance. Occupying forces are being withdrawn. The drones are being sent in."

Abraham caught a glimpse of his son's reaction. Iniko's eyes were wide for a moment, but he regained control of himself the next instant.

Abraham said nothing. He nodded his head. He wasn't hiding anything. He understood the inevitability of the cities destruction long before the man sitting next to him. He was unaffected by the news.

As the night continued, Abraham watched and listened to Sarah as she played her role in his escape plan. She smiled, laughed at the boy's crass jokes, grabbed their biceps pretending to be impressed. To one of the boys she said, "There must be droves of women waiting for you to come home." To another she said, "A girl would be lucky to meet a man like you." To Farrow she said, "I love men who take charge." She kept this up all night. The boys, all with the same object in mind, cancelled each other's efforts as they vied for position. They all thought they had a chance, unaware that Sarah was not at all, an object to be won; rather, the subject causing these mere boys to act according to her will.

To each of the boys she promised, "Tomorrow night, I will come to you. Tonight I must be with my son." She gave no additional explanation.

Before going to sleep she exclaimed loudly, "Goodnight you brave men. I rest easy knowing that I am surrounded by such virtuous gentlemen." With this she went to her tent. She had set it up with the help of Iniko earlier that day. He followed her. Sarah could hear the men boasting. She held the grip of the revolver tightly in her hand.

Darkness surrounded the camp. The fire had gone out long ago. Night was almost over. A shadow lurked unseen. It belonged to the only man still awake.

Abraham had pretended to go to sleep. After the last man had retired to his hammock, Abraham continued to wait. For his plan to work he needed for everyone to be asleep.

The shadow descended on its first victim. The victim was lying stomach up in a hammock. Abraham covered the mouth of the victim while pressing the knife to the throat. With a sawing motion he opened the arteries. The man in the hammock struggled helplessly, but the grip of Abraham was strong.

The second victim was Earl. He was sprawled out on a

foam pad. The knife went directly through his left eye socket. No sound escaped.

The third victim was in a hammock like the first. Just as Abraham reached for his mouth, he woke up. Too startled to scream, the victim gasped inaudibly. Before he could call out, a strong hand was upon his throat, and the knife was plunged deep in his chest.

The fourth victim was in a hammock. His mouth was covered. His arteries were opened.

There were three left. All three were in tents. Abraham unzipped the first tent as quietly as he could. The man inside was not quite snoring. He was breathing loudly. When Abraham entered the tent, the man woke up. He screamed. Abraham had to act quickly. He dove at the man stabbing at his body indiscriminately. In the struggle, the tent collapsed.

The man did not go quietly. He punched, kicked, and bit. With a final thrust of the knife the man quit fighting.

Abraham cut his way out of the tent to find two men. Farrow was standing next to the other remaining deserter. The unnamed deserter was carrying a rail gun.

"Drop the knife," Farrow said, "we're not going to kill you just yet. You killed my men. I'm going to make this hurt."

The loud pop was not that of a rail gun. Abraham heard the sound, and he saw the man carrying the rail gun fall over. He landed on his side. A large exit wound could be seen in his head.

Sarah stepped forward.

"We took you in;" Farrow said, "we let you into our camp. Why?"

She fired her revolver and Farrow fell to the ground dead.

"Well, that's it for tonight my boy," the old storyteller said as he stood up in front of the dying embers of the fire. He yawned. The olive skin of his wrinkled hand covered his heavily bearded mouth. In the darkness, the boy could see that the crystal blue eyes had become drowsy. That night, he knew better than to ask for more.

"Good," the boy began to say yawning, "night."

"More tomorrow," the old man said as he walked towards the ground that he had previously prepared to sleep on.

CHAPTER III

For the second day in a row, the journey was uneventful. The boy began to feel relaxed around his new traveling companions. He began to forget those that he had recently lost.

He did not do this coldly. This was his life. Like an animal, he had learned to love those around him, and to simply forget those that he no longer saw in front of him.

The group set up camp early that night.

"No fire tonight," one of the men said, "not here."

At this the boy was disappointed. The men went to sleep early on nights such as this. "Don't worry little friend," the old storyteller said. "Come out on this rock with me, we'll watch the sun go down and I'll tell you the next part of my story."

The storyteller put his hand on the boy's shoulder and picked up where he left off the night before.

When the family awoke, late in the morning, they found themselves surrounded by death. Sarah was the first to notice the buzzards circling overhead. There was no discussion of burying the dead. "A generous offering," she said to herself. "They'll eat for weeks."

Abraham overheard and considered this for a moment. Soberly he said, "I doubt that. These are not the only animals that feast upon the dead in this wilderness. We're far away from the road and these woods are less forgiving than those that we have traveled for recreation."

Understanding him, Sarah began to gather the family's gear into bags. "Iniko," she said, "I want you to pack our bags. Your father and I are going to take a look through the cave. The deserters may have had things that we can use."

"Ok," Iniko responded, doing everything he could to hold back his fear.

In the cave Abraham said to Sarah, "I want to grab as many of these boxes as we can."

"How much ammunition are we going to need?" Sarah asked.

"Enough to supply us for the rest of our lives if we can carry it. We have their truck now. We can probably carry all of it. If we can get it up to Church Peak."

"Alright," Sarah responded as she placed her hands on the handles of the first aluminum crate. Abraham grabbed the handles on the other side and they lifted together. Out of the cave but only half way to the truck Sarah said, "my hand is slipping." They put down the crate. She took a breath. "Alright," she said after another moment. They picked up the crate and carried it towards the closed back hatch of the truck. Abraham tried the handle. It was locked.

"Hmm," he said.

"Farrow had them," Sarah said in answer.

"Right," Abraham responded. He walked over to Farrow's dead body. In the eyes, there was still the affectation of surprise. Abraham felt no remorse. He left the eyes open wide as he reached into the dead man's left pocket. He found a small knife but the keys were not there. He reached into the right pocket and pulled out a small plastic object. He pressed the small red button and heard the locks of the truck disengage.

"He had them," Abraham said to Sarah as he opened the back hatch. Abraham and Sarah both groaned as they heaved the heavy box of ammunition into the back of the truck.

"Ready for the next one?" Abraham said.

"Can you move the truck closer?" she responded.

"Yea." Abraham opened the driver side door of the truck. The truck was designed for off road driving. It was entirely manual. It was not driverless. He pressed the power button without noticing the battery level. His thoughts were too focused on the ammunition. He was thinking of his future safety and security on top of Church Peak.

"You can come back a little further," Sarah said to Abraham as he backed up the truck. "That's good, stop."

Back in the cave, Abraham and Sarah picked up the next box of ammunition. "I think they'll all fit," she said.

"I think so."

When the eighth and final box was loaded, Sarah sat down on a stump next to the fire ring and wiped the sweat from her brow. She breathed heavily, watching Abraham as he loaded additional rail guns, and handguns into the truck. Iniko walked over to her.

"The bags are packed," he said.

"Thank you my son." She replied.

"That's a lot of guns," he remarked.

"That's a lot of guns," she said in response.

With the truck loaded Abraham took one last look at the campsite. A thin stream of smoke danced lazily above the smoldering remains of the campfire. Two buzzards, the bravest of the group had landed next to the body of one of the boys who had been killed in the night. One of the birds was very close indeed. Abraham turned back towards his family before he could witness the sharp beak plunge towards its natural destination.

"Iniko," Abraham said, "I want you to sit in the back." The boy nodded his head, opened the door of the truck, pulled himself up into the seat and sat down. He shut the door, buckled his seat belt, and looked ahead.

"Well, Abraham," Sarah said coyly, "What's the plan?"

"It shouldn't be too much trouble getting back out onto the road," he said in response. "I paid close attention as we drove out."

"Then what?"

"To Church Peak, "Abraham answered, "I think that's our safest option. Did you hear Farrow last night?"

"No."

"The city," he said, "it's anarchy. Farrow made it sound like something happened a couple days ago. Drones are being sent."

"You were right. It's funny. I never doubted you; I trusted you from the first, but I'm still surprised."

Abraham smiled and kissed his wife on the mouth. "It seems that we're in one of those unique situations where our path is set. We can only move forward from here."

"I trust you."

Abraham and Sarah got in the truck. As he pulled out of the encampment, he didn't think to look down at the control panel. Perhaps he was still brimming with emotion from the tender moment he had just shared with his wife. Who knows? What is certain is that if he had, he would have noticed that the electricity left in the car battery was dangerously low.

Shortly after pulling out of the encampment, Sarah was struck with an idea. She pressed a button on the console and a voice filled the speakers of the truck.

'...the announcement was made early this morning. The city was razed to the ground last night in a coordinated drone strike orchestrated through the cooperation of allied forces. The strike was the result of the national governments complete inability to control its populace. It was the last resort after months of negotiations.

'For an entire week before the strike, the populace had descended into anarchy. Footage taken over the past week, which has been shown all over the web, demonstrates clearly the perils of foreign sovereignty. And that is why it has been our duty...'

Sarah could not listen to any more. She looked over towards Abraham, whose expression showed nearly as much confusion as her own. "A whole week?" she asked.

Abraham did not answer her right away. They sat in silence for almost half an hour. He looked back towards Iniko once. The boy appeared more frightened now then he had when the family was first confronted by Farrow.

The road was just in sight when he finally asked

rhetorically, "Was that a foreign station? Those have been blocked for years."

"Not in this truck," Sarah said, "this truck is foreign too. They were deserters."

"It makes you wonder," Abraham replied, "How…" but was cut short by a strange sensation in his right foot. The pressure from the accelerator had suddenly ceased entirely. He pushed his foot all the way down and felt nothing. The truck gradually began to slow. It was in this moment that Abraham thought to look down towards the control panel. The battery was dead.

As an old impulse, Abraham slammed the palm of his hand down on the steering wheel, for helplessness is the great propagator of senseless violence. He did this twice more. Sarah let out a sigh of disbelief. Her eyes showed fear.

Iniko began to cry, his sobs stifled by the remaining force of his will.

The truck stopped entirely and Abraham got out and slammed the door behind him. He walked right out in the midst of the arid grasses and shrubs. He walked over a hundred steps away from the car and stood looking out into the empty horizon. Above him the sun was red hot. The ground was dust. The thorny branches of shrubberies had torn open the skin of his forearms. One of the cuts was deep. A drop of blood trickled down towards his fingertips, its gravity nearly causing it to detach and fall crashing to the ground.

He pulled that arm up. His eyes searched the deep scratch

on his outer forearm. With his tongue he licked the blood. He walked back to the truck to find the nervous eyes of Iniko and the fear that had taken over the body of his wife. Both Sarah and Iniko had gotten out of the truck and were standing behind it.

Abraham let out a deep breath and with this the features of his wife softened. Iniko's shoulders, which had been drawn up towards his ears, relaxed. "We can't go back for another battery," Abraham said. "It would be almost three days walk each way and there would be no guarantee that the truck would still be here when we got back. Even if it was guaranteed, it'd be too dangerous to go back to the camp anyway. With us gone, who knows what'll come to finish those bodies."

Iniko, happy that his father didn't name the animals that prey on the dead, nodded his head as his mother said, "ok."

"From here I say we trek our way to Church Peak. We'll carry the same packs we had before with four magazines of ammunition each. Sarah, you and I will carry a rail gun each. I want you to give the revolver to Iniko. That's the only gun he's ever shot. He knows how to use it. You and I can strap a couple of these handguns to our thighs."

"Ok," Sarah replied, her head turning back toward the truck. From above the rear window she could see the cases of ammunition stacked nearly to the ceiling. Feeling the soreness in her arms from the lifting of those boxes that morning, she walked over and opened the hatch. Abraham followed her. Together they pulled down a crate. Using his knife, Abraham opened it. Together they pulled out twelve magazines of ammunition and left the rest in the box.

And so it was that Abraham, heavily laden with food, supplies, and ammunition abandoned the truck and began the long journey south towards the abandoned hotel at Church Peak. The stockpile of ammunition, the extra camping supplies, and the extra tent were left behind. On his back, and on the backs of his wife and child were worn the supplies that they could collectively carry. Everything they owned.

If the family could have stayed there, in that spot, they would have, but their needs for food were more than their backs could bear. Rations for five days, water for two was all that was left. On each of their backs, the weight equaling that of a young boy pulled them down towards the Earth. It was hot, and that was a lot of weight to carry for a young man such as Iniko. It was a lot of weight for a young man who doesn't complain, a young man who would sooner fall behind than disappoint his father.

"Well," the old storyteller said to the young boy, "it is dark. It would be best to get some rest."

"I couldn't sleep now," the boy said in response.

"I suppose I couldn't either," the storyteller said.

"I have a question," the young boy said, "there was a voice in the truck. How could that be? Whose voice was that?"

The storyteller smiled. "You are a young one," he said laughing, "You have never heard of the men talk of the radio?"

"No."

It was common for the men and women of these wandering groups to speak of the ancient technology of their youths. Men would remember the screens on which they watched football. Women might remember the phones they spoke through. For most, these were second hand memories. The storyteller, however, was a young man at the time of the catastrophe. He had known how life was before the fall.

"The radio, the flatscreen," the storyteller answered, "that was how our people communicated through very long distances. A man could speak in one part of the world, and another man could hear him on the other side of the world. That is what the radio did. There was a radio in the truck. The man speaking was telling the news. Just like a storyteller will tell a story."

"I see."

"Well," the old man said, "If you don't mind the dark, I don't mind the dark. There is still much story to tell."

It was early in the afternoon when the family began walking towards the road. The walk was a gentle slope up a wide trail formed by the repeated contact of the deserter's truck tires with the ground. It was late in the afternoon when Abraham recognized where he was. Sarah recognized it in the same moment.

"That's our car," she said in surprise.

"We must have taken a different road."

Iniko, silent, his muscles aching from the additional burden, couldn't hide his dismay. He put his pack down where he stood and began to cry into his hands.

Sarah, still wearing her pack, placed her hands on her hips and said, "I didn't see it turn off."

Abraham, his lips pursed, replied, "No. Neither did I." He shook his head. "Just a day and a half gone." His lips tightened as he stared off into the distance.

Sarah bent over Iniko. "Did you hear your father? We just lost a day in a half. In six days we'll be there. It's ok."

Iniko dropped his hands away from his eyes. His eyes were deeply reddened. He looked up at his father who was still staring off into the distance. He must have wondered at his father's appearance, for this man, cool, calm, was nothing like the father he had grown up with. He stood up and picked up his pack.

"That's better," Sarah said. "It's going to be ok," she said. She said this but she knew it meant nothing.

Iniko walked over to his father placing his hand on his elbow. Abraham turned his head down towards his son to see the red already fading from his eyes and a smile, a genuine smile on his lips.

When they finally reached the car, it was beginning to get dark.

"I can't believe it," Abraham exclaimed. "It's still here. He put down his pack and walked towards the altar that he had built after the car had flipped over into the ditch. It was nothing but blackened earth. The kindling had burned down to nothing. The ID cards that he had placed in the center had melted completely. "Iniko," Abraham shouted out towards his son, "Get your pack off and help me get together some wood."

With the wood piled up, Abraham struck a match. He was about to light the pile when Sarah said, "No, wait!" Abraham stood with the match burning towards his fingertips. "Abraham, don't light that."

"What's the matter?" Abraham said curiously.

"The deserters," Sarah replied, "what if there are more."

Abraham was struck with an awareness that had eluded his imagination since the beginning of their flight. He blew out the match.

About to speak, Abraham caught Iniko's eye. He held his son's worried glance for several moments before turning back towards Sarah. "I doubt more than one band of deserters could be here. They'd end up killing each other. No, those were the only ones." Sarah, in this moment looked worried, but Iniko didn't notice. He was looking at his father intently. "But," Abraham continued, "You're right Sarah; we shouldn't light it." Sarah let out a deep breath. "It would be better," Abraham said, "to leave it here as an altar."

Sarah, now playing along said, "Oh, an altar to what?"

"Why, to ourselves of course and no-one else," he said mirthfully, "now, what would you two like to dine on tonight?"

He reached into the bag and pulled out three meal bars and a bottle of water. "We have meal bars and water."

Iniko slept soundly that night as his parents, in whispers, discussed the real dangers that they were sure to face.

"And that's all tonight my boy," the storyteller said. "When Abraham goes to sleep, I go to sleep."

"So he was able to sleep that night? What were the dangers? Are they the same..."

"Now boy," the storyteller said cutting him off, "those questions are off limits. You'll find out when we get to that part of the story. Goodnight my boy."

The storyteller stood up, stretched, and found a place to sleep in the grass. The boy curled up on the dark, flat rock that was still warm from the rays of the day's sun.

CHAPTER IV

It was late in the afternoon when the group was ambushed by three men wielding sharpened sticks. The boy was the target; it was almost always the young boys and girls who were. To our ears this sounds horrific, but only because these were men and not animals.

After all, the young are commonly preyed upon in nature. Many species of animal, under strained conditions, will resort to cannibalism. And as much as we hate to admit it, that has been true within our species as well.

The group could have let the poachers, that was the term generally used, take the boy without a fight. This was common practice. But that did not happen. This group had been together for many, many years. The storyteller stood fast next to the boy. A spear was hurled. It missed its target. Another poacher made a mad dash to grab at the boy, but one of the younger men was there to meet his advances.

The poacher thrust his spear but caught only air. In

another moment he was on the ground, his head smashed in with a club.

The poachers were now outnumbered four to two. They had lost the advantage of surprise. The poacher, who had retained his spear, threw his projectile at the boy. It was thrown well. It was thrown on target. If not for the storyteller, the boy would have been impaled. Just before the tip of the spear could strike its target, the storyteller, using his staff, knocked the projectile out of the air. In the same moment, another man from the group threw a large stone, large enough to shatter a man's skull on impact. With a loud thud, the stone struck the first spear throwing poacher on the side of the head. He fell lifeless to the ground.

Other stones were thrown, but each missed its mark. The third poacher ran off into the thick vegetation of the forest.

Later that night a large fire was built. It was suspected that the attack earlier was the work of three desperate men and nothing else. For years this had been safe territory. For years the organized bands of poachers had stayed away from here. After some discussion it was decided that the attack was singular and a fire could be built.

The group ate well. When the meal was over and most of the group asleep, the old man sat next to the boy, the fire warm on his leathery skin. Flames darted up towards the moonless, starry sky. He pulled out his knife, a large heavy knife, and held the blade in the palm of his hand. With his thumb and forefinger he grasped the tip of blade tightly. Using only the tip, he scraped at the space between two of his top teeth. The meat that had been wedged between his teeth, causing considerable discomfort, came out onto the tip of the knife. He took this piece of cooked flesh and flicked it into the fire.

"My boy!" the storyteller said laughing heartily, "You had quite the scare today. But you still seem yourself."

"It's happened before," he replied earnestly, "since I was little, it's always happened. One day, I'll be unlucky. That's what happens."

The old man saw the absence of fear in the boy's eyes. "But that is not the way it always will be. We will outlast them. They cannot live forever like this. Our people will survive."

"OK," the boy said innocently. "So, will you keep telling the story? Will you tell me the rest?"

Startled, the storyteller answered, "Yes, why, I wasn't sure you'd be up to it, but yes, where did I leave off?"

"When Abraham found the car. He found the altar but he didn't light it."

"That's right. It was too dangerous."

After an almost sleepless night, Abraham woke to find that his wife, child, and supplies were all still in his possession. He was greatly relieved.

He roused Iniko first. "Have some water and a meal bar." He said to his son.

He woke his wife, who sat straight up, eyes wide, searching

the surrounding landscape. She yawned deeply, stood up and began packing the camping supplies. When all three had eaten breakfast, Abraham picked up his pack. He hoisted the weight onto his stiff shoulders and looked back once at the altar. "To ourselves, and no-one else," he said and began walking down the road.

For the first half of the day, Iniko stayed close to his parents. Some of the time he held his mother's hand. "What will it be like?" he asked while the sun was still low in the sky.

"Beautiful," she answered, "much more beautiful than the city. It is on the top of a mountain but within a shallow valley. The gardens are full of flowers. The grass is a green you have never before seen with your eyes. And the hotel. We'll have it all to ourselves." At this, Abraham turned towards Sarah with an unconscious expression of concern. "An entire hotel to ourselves," she said.

Iniko asked how big the hotel was.

"Oh," Sarah replied turning her head towards Abraham, "how big would you say?"

Abraham considered this seriously, "I think I remember there being over a hundred rooms," he said.

"That sounds about right," Sarah rejoined.

Iniko compared the size of the hotel to the size of the apartment building that the family had lived in.

"Not quite that large," Abraham replied, "but close."

Iniko was mesmerized. "But what if someone else wants to live there? What if there's another family out there just like ours? Do you think we're the only ones that escaped?"

Abraham turned towards Sarah. He was uneasy. About to speak, Abraham turned towards the road in front of him and decided to say nothing.

Sarah answered her son's question, "Well," she said, "We had neighbors in the apartment didn't we?"

"Yea," Iniko answered, "all my friends were there."

"Well," Sarah said, "don't you think it will be ok if we have neighbors at the hotel?"

Iniko shook his head. "Maybe I'll meet other kids there. Maybe some of my friends are going too."

"We'll just have to see," Sarah said smiling, catching a glimpse of Abraham's uneasy eyes.

When the sun reached the top of the sky, Abraham turned back towards Sarah and Iniko. Wife and son, holding hands, smiled up towards Abraham. He nodded his head in the direction of the brush and walked down the hill off of the highway. Behind two large boulders, the smaller leaning up against the larger, Abraham dropped his pack. He pulled the pistol that was harnessed to his right thigh out of the holster and laid it on the ground within hands reach.

"How do you feel?" he asked Iniko seriously as the boy put his pack down and sat with his back leaning against the larger of the two boulders.

"Better than yesterday," the child answered, "I'm thirsty."

Sarah had already taken a long drink from the water bottle. She passed it to Iniko, who drank greedily from the bottle.

Abraham pulled out a second water bottle and three meal bars. Under the shadow of the boulders, the family ate lunch. Sarah began to sing a song that she and Abraham had sung to Iniko when he was only an infant. At the chorus, exactly as he had years ago, Abraham harmonized with his wife.

When the song was over, they sang another. Iniko did not know the words. Within memory he had never heard the songs sung. It was as if he could feel the tune, the emotions were there, something was there, but the words were undefined. He hummed along in tune, the ancient memory floating weightlessly, untouchably around him.

As the sun began to fall back towards the Earth, Abraham stood up and looked in every direction. Sarah, seeing that Iniko was about to stand, grabbed him by the waist and pulled him back down towards the ground. She forced down his arms with her knees. "No," he cried, "No, don't, mom, don't!"

With her fingers she found his exposed ribs. "No," he cried, "don't!"

It was too late. Iniko began laughing uncontrollably, "don't, mom, d…"

Abraham, standing above his wife laughed heartily. In a movement he had her under her arms.

"No," Sarah squealed, "no," she said one last time. She fell to the ground limp. Iniko, now recovered, joined the onslaught finding the space on the underside of her knee.

"I'll pee," she said, but Abraham nor Iniko heeded this warning. It was a bluff. It was always a bluff. "I give, I give... Abe."

"Alright," Abraham said. Iniko had already stopped. "I'm being nice this time."

Sarah stood up cautiously, her elbows down at her sides guarding her ribs and eyeing her family suspiciously.

With his hands in front of him, Abraham bucked towards Sarah. "Ah," she screamed as she took a quick step backwards. "Don't."

She reached down towards her pack keeping both eyes on Abraham. Iniko had already put on his pack.

Abraham eyed his wife.

"Devious," she said.

After several moments more, Abraham turned around and picked up his pack. With this, the family headed back up towards the highway.

During the second half of the day, Abraham and Sarah walked together. Iniko kept back ten paces. He was old enough to know that his parents wanted to talk. He followed along silently working hard to keep up with his parents' longer legs and stronger frames.

As the afternoon wore on and a haze settled on the outer edge of the horizon obscuring the vision and perceptiveness of the family, Abraham began to talk very seriously to Sarah about his concerns.

"There must be others out here," Abraham said without turning towards his wife.

"They'd be in the same place as us," Sarah replied reassuring herself.

"Maybe," Abraham said. He and Sarah walked on without speaking.

Meanwhile, Iniko's steps became heavier. His chin sunk down to his chest. He was not watching the horizon. He was no longer watching the figures of his parents walking in front of him. His eyes, unfocused, followed the patterns of footsteps on the ground. The eyes followed but did not focus. Sweat ran down the back of his neck. His shirt was not damp. It was wet. Even so, he did not utter a single cry of complaint. He trudged along, gradually falling behind, looking down, he did not notice that he was falling behind.

From a distance, he would have appeared like the calf of a nomadic beast. Like a young elephant or steer on the move during a drought, his legs appeared weak. He was trembling and falling behind and no-one noticed.
Trembling and falling behind yet so exhausted and ignorant of the surrounding dangers that he did not notice himself.
All the while, the animals of prey were in the bushes. The

animals of prey were waiting for the perfect moment, to kill without warning or notice to the parents whose eyes were looking forward.

It was a long time before Abraham again spoke. "What if, "he said ponderously, "what if we ran out of food? What if we were out here and couldn't find water? What would you be willing to do?"

Sarah shook her head.

"What if it meant Iniko's life?"

She continued to shake her head, "No, Abraham, I wouldn't. I would never. Even then."

"But," Abraham said, "the guards, the deserters, you had no qualms then."

"They had no right. They would have killed us. But the innocent. I would never harm the innocent."

"You wouldn't," Abraham said with darkness in his eyes, "I know you wouldn't. But I know others would."

Abraham and Sarah continued to walk, looking forward, too rapt in thought to look back.

"We should be careful about where we camp," Sarah said, "If we just get off the road like we did for lunch, I think we'll be safe."

"At night," Abraham replied, "I'm worried about fires."

"The fire keeps the animals away," Sarah said. "I don't

know much about it. We never camped or hiked here. But from what I've heard, it can be dangerous at night. Last night I was against having a fire, but I've been thinking. I think we would be better off if we had one tonight."

"We'll keep fires small," Abraham answered. "Not like our first night."

"What difference does it make?" Sarah said. "Out here, what difference does it make? Anyone within a day's walk can see a small fire out here."

Abraham nodded his head. She was exaggerating but her point was made.

"There are real dangers out here that we know of. Those take precedent over those that are only suspected."

Abraham nodded. "For now," he said and nothing else.

Further behind, with the distance growing, Iniko realized that the forms of his parents had shrunk considerably. For a few steps he tried to move faster. For a few steps he went through the motions of catching his parents. He gave it up. "The road is straight," he said to himself out loud. "I'll be able to see them no matter how far they get ahead. It'll be time to camp soon," he thought hopefully. All of this was said out loud, but Abraham and Sarah were too far ahead to hear it.

"Remember that time," Abraham said to Sarah, "we were trail running in the U.A. Remember that old couple that was walking in front of us. They were talking so loudly to each other. They were talking so loud they didn't hear us. I called out 'on your left,' so we could pass them."

At this Sarah began to laugh. This was a favorite story for Abraham to tell. It was a comfort story. The type of story he told to feel good.

"That old lady shrieked so loud, must of thought I was a bear."

"I thought the old guy was gonna turn around and knock you on the head," Sarah said.

"He wasn't happy." Abraham agreed.

In the same moment, Sarah realized that she hadn't turned around to check on Iniko since they left for lunch. She looked over her shoulder. She stopped walking. She turned around and dropped her pack.

Abraham stopped walking. Looking over his shoulder, he could see Sarah running back down the road.

"Iniko!" Sarah screamed. "Iniko!"

Abraham dropped his pack. "Iniko!" he called. "Iniko!" But his son did not answer. With his eyes, Abraham searched the horizon. The highway, still hazy from the warm afternoon sun, was empty except for the running figure of Sarah.

"Where is he?" Sarah howled. "Where?"

The highway went north and south. Abraham scanned the horizon east of the road. He scanned the west. In the distance, to the west Abraham could see movement in a bush.

On the road he could see Sarah stooped down. He ran to her.

"His water bottle," she said desperately. It's here. No, Abraham, no. Something. Something got our son."

"There's movement in the bushes. Out there," Abraham replied pointing his finger to the west. Abraham was holding his rail gun with his other hand.

Sarah pulled out the pistol from the holster on her right thigh. Together they plunged into the brush leaving their packs and the other rail gun behind.

The chase was on. Leaping over brush, running through the defensive spines of shrubberies, Abraham and Sarah had nothing to guide their movement through the wilderness aside from the original swaying of a tall shrub in the distance. Sarah, who had gotten ahead, ran for that shrub. Abraham, slightly behind and to the left ran for a point just beyond it.

Spines ripped flesh as Sarah ran heeding nothing but the tall shrub in the distance. Abraham moved cautiously. Keeping up, but watching the ground in front of him.

Then, suddenly, the fixed point in the distance no longer mattered. A stifled scream, the scream of a child whose mouth was covered but had bitten the hand, rang out across the prairie.

"Iniko," Sarah called unwisely. Before that moment, the

kidnapper hadn't noticed his pursuers.

Abraham swung wide to the left of the voice. Sarah ran right at it.

Another scream could be heard, this time much closer. "Mom!" The kidnapper hadn't expected this. The boy was still wearing his pack. Pulling the boy, who kept falling over his own feet, the kidnapper's progress was slow indeed.

Sarah could see him now. She ran right through a thorny shrub feeling nothing. She raised her pistol, "Stop," she howled, "stop."

The man, balding and overweight turned around with one arm holding Iniko in front of him. At the end of the other arm, in his hand was the ancient revolver. It was pointed at Sarah. He pulled the trigger. It wouldn't pull. It was stuck. He looked down at the revolver. With his thumb he disengaged the safety. He pointed the revolver at Sarah.

Sarah didn't move. She aimed the pistol at the kidnapper. She looked into his sunken grey eyes. His bald, uncovered head was bright red from overexposure to the sun. The dark hair that formed a horseshoe around his skull was only slightly disheveled. His paunch hung out over the waistline of his heavily worn trousers.

Fear, he stank of fear. He couldn't make eye contact with Sarah. His hand, with the revolver at its end shook terribly.

Sarah stood still as a pillar. Her hand was steady. Iniko was shaking. He was crying, but she did not see.

The blast from the revolver was loud. Sarah didn't move. A second blast filled the air with sound.

In the same moment, Abraham emerged on the kidnapper's right flank. Startled by the sudden appearance of Abraham, who had never called out to his son, the kidnapper fell over, losing his grip of Iniko and dropping the revolver.

Iniko, free from kidnappers grip ran a few steps, stumbled over his feet and landed face first on the ground.

The kidnapper reached for the revolver. It was in his fingertips when another blast filled the dry, acrid air. With her left eye closed, with the sights still aligned, Sarah watched through the thin smoke drifting up from the barrel of her pistol, as the kidnapper groaned and writhed on the ground. He was no longer reaching for the revolver. He held his gut as blood flowed out, staining his shirt and forming a shallow puddle in the place where he lay. "I wouldn't of…" he hissed, his fork tongue protruding slightly from his drawn lips. "I wasn't going to." He said nothing else as the puddle gradually seeped into the cracks of the earth.

Sarah walked up to the man who was still groaning. His face was filled with the grotesque machinations of muscles contorting uncontrollably with pain. His jaw, clenched tightly looked like the jowls of a snake. She aimed the pistol at his head. She held it there as she scrutinized the wound that she had inflicted. "Out here," she said aloud but to herself, "given time, he will most assuredly die." She allowed the pistol to drop to her side. She returned it to its holster on her right thigh.

Abraham looked on as his wife helped Iniko up to his feet. She dusted him off, kissed his forehead. She looked into her son's eyes with tears in her own.

Iniko trembled. He continued to do so even when his mother's arms were around him, holding him as tightly as she could.

Abraham was in the same place that he had been when he surprised the kidnapper. His eyes fell down towards the man who had stolen his son. 'Why,' he wondered. "What was your purpose," he muttered to himself. "What did he say," Abraham said still muttering, "what was it? 'I wouldn't of,' that was it. I wouldn't have what? Killed him? What was his purpose?" Abraham's eyes traveled back to his wife and son. Iniko was no longer trembling. He stood awkwardly with his mother's arms around him and his pack protruding from his back.

"Shit," Abraham bawled loudly. "Shit, the packs. He wasn't alone. They're after the packs."

Running back through the brush, in a line, straight for the road, Abraham hurtled dense clumps of brush allowing thorns to tear the skin of his arms and cheeks. This time he could see a man and a woman. The couple had just lifted the packs off the ground. The rail gun that Sarah had left was in neither of their hands.

Abraham kept running with his eyes on the couple. He saw the woman point in his direction. A moment later, the man scurried over to the place where Sarah had left her rail gun. He picked up the weapon and pointed it towards Abraham.

Catching up, yet still far behind, Sarah ran with Iniko holding his right hand. In her right hand she held the revolver that she had picked up off the ground after Abraham had realized the ambushers true intentions.

Sarah and Iniko were slow to catch up. The pair was encumbered by Iniko's heavy pack. Iniko by now was exhausted.

Abraham aimed his rail gun at the man in the road. He did not fire. "Put it down," Abraham yelled. "Just put it down. We don't have to do this."

The man in the road closed his left eye. "I'll put it down if you put yours down," he said loudly, without screaming.

Abraham aimed at the man's chest. "Just put it down!" he yelled.

"Adam Lot," the big, dark man said loudly still pointing his rail gun towards Abraham. Both eyes were open now.

"This here's my wife." The woman, petit and fair skinned bowed her head slightly. She smiled.

Abraham made no reply. He held his aim at the center of the large man's chest.

"There is no need for this," the big man said. "We have your supplies, yes, but you've killed our friend. Why let this quarrel continue? Why should there be strife when your supplies are so many, and of you, there are only three?"

Abraham said nothing.

"End this standoff and agree. We'll take one bag. You take the other. It is fair. It is more than fair. You're boy still has his bag, and you have blood on your hands. This is how it is done out here. There is no need for killing. After all, we are brethren in like condition."

As the big man finished this speech, Sarah and Iniko, breathing hard, caught up to Abraham. Seeing the rail gun pointed in the direction of her husband, Sarah ushered Iniko to the ground. She told him to lay flat as she loaded two bullets into the revolver from a pouch that she wore on her hip. She aimed the revolver at the man on the road.

"Agree," the big man said again, "enough blood has been spilt. Do it thus. Point in the direction that you would travel. Just point with your weapon. Point right, and we will go left. Point left, and we will go right. We will take one bag and drop the other." The big man's wife dropped the pack that she was carrying. "See," the big man said, "our part has been done. The whole land is open to you. We are brothers in this. We should not fight."

The big man lowered the stolen rail gun. Abraham squeezed the trigger. The projectile from Abraham's rail gun smashed into the big man's chest knocking him off his feet. He was dead before he hit the ground. His fair skinned wife, in a rage, picked up the rail gun that had dropped to the dead man's side. She picked up the weapon but did not raise it to her shoulder. Her eyes covered the vast track between herself and Abraham. She could see Abraham, who held his weapon with a steady aim. She dropped the gun and squatted over the dead body of her late husband.

Sarah told Iniko to stay where he was. With Abraham she walked up towards the road. She kept her revolver raised towards the cowering body of the fair skinned woman.

The woman was still crying over her dead husband when Abraham and Sarah took their first steps back up on the road.

"Get up," Abraham said with authority.

She did not get up at first. A few moments passed and she turned around still squatting. She sat down on the road and said despairingly, "you monsters. You killed him. You killed them."

Abraham said nothing at first. Then, with authority, he said, "get up."

"Just one pack. That was all we wanted. One pack. You don't need all this. You don't need all this."

"Get up," was how he replied.

"One pack," she said, "ours were taken just like this. That's how it is out here. You didn't need to." She started crying. Her face reddened as the tears flowed down.

Sarah started to show irritation. "It was never one pack. You would have taken everything if you could. You would have killed our son. You'd have killed all three of us if it meant your survival. It was never one pack. Now get up before I shoot you in the head."

The desperate figure, fawnlike, stood up with the tears still streaming down. "Let me go with you," she said desperately towards Abraham. "Please, I hated him anyway. I hated them both. The man that took your son, he made us do it. It was his idea. He was terrible to me. He did things. Let me go with you."

"No," Abraham said evenly.

The fair skinned woman was wearing a white hiking shirt. 'Evelyn' was embroidered on the left breast pocket. Long, light colored hiking pants covered her legs. Her head was covered with a wide brimmed hat. Her face was reddened from crying, not from sunburn.

Her eyes, still full of tears fixed on the pack that she had dropped. "Please," she said, "I didn't know. I didn't know it to be evil. When I stole the pack, I didn't know."

"You knew," Abraham said evenly, "it had happened to you, so you knew. You would have had us stripped of our belongings in a wilderness. Our property, you would have stolen it and felt no remorse. You lie now, you manufacture these tears with the same purpose."

Suddenly, the eyes of the fair skinned woman sharpened. The tears stopped. A mischievous smile filled her countenance. "I would kill you in the night," she said venomously.

"Strip," Abraham replied.

Surprised, Sarah caught Abraham's eye.

"Everything," Abraham said, "take off everything."

Evelyn took off her hat obediently. She unbuttoned her

shirt and placed it delicately on top of the hat. She took off her boots and let them stay in the place that she had taken them off. She took off her socks and pants. She stood before Abraham and Sarah without covering her body.

"Everything," Abraham said.

Evelyn took off her undergarments. She did not hide her body.

"You'll walk north," Abraham said. "You'll walk in the middle of the road until it gets dark. This weapon can fire very long distances. If you turn around I'll shoot. If you stop walking straight I'll shoot. If you stop walking, I'll shoot. After today, if I ever see you again, I'll shoot."

Evelyn was still smiling mischievously. She turned around and began walking north. Her proud form straightened as she took her first steps. Her arms swung loosely at her sides. Her wide hips swayed. Her pale, white skin contrasted the dark black of the open road. The sun shined off her skin. The road burned the heels of her feet.

Abraham peered through the scope of his rail gun. He kept the crosshairs on the center of her back.

"The man," Sarah said to Abraham, "Adam Lot. Was it his intention to deceive us? Did you have no choice?"

"No," Abraham answered, "he did not deceive. He was afraid, but his intentions of robbing us were clear. He made no direct threat on our lives, but his intention of robbing us was clear."

"That was enough?"

Abraham did not answer. He kept the crosshairs on the fair woman's back. "Get Iniko," he said. "Can you roll over the dead man? We need that pack."

"I'll get the pack first," she replied. Sarah bent over the dead man and rolled him on his side. She slipped his right arm through the pack strap. She rolled him back and on his other side. She slipped his left arm through the pack strap. She rolled him on his stomach and removed the pack.

There was a large quantity of blood that had soaked into the padding of the pack. There was a small hole in the pack where the projectile had entered.

Sarah opened the pack to check its contents. She pulled everything out. There was a large hole in a pair of pants. There was a hole in a shirt and a small hole on the outside of the pack. Nothing important was damaged. The man's blood had not seeped into the interior of the pack. Only the padding was wet.

When Sarah found Iniko, he was lying against his pack.

"Are you ok," she asked.

"I'm glad you didn't hurt her," Iniko said.

Sarah let this go and allowed him to feel this way. She helped him to his feet. He picked up his pack and walked up to the road smiling.

Abraham was still aiming his rail gun when Sarah and Iniko walked up to his side. He held it this way with the fair skinned woman in his cross hairs until the sun touched the western horizon.

"We'll walk down the road until dark and camp in the brush," Abraham said as he allowed his rail gun to fall to his side. He put the gun down and stretched his shoulders. He tried to pick up his pack with his left arm but could not. His left hand was shaking. His left arm was sore from holding the rail gun for so long. He picked up his pack with his right arm, which was not so sore, and led his family to a camping spot that was well hidden amongst the brush. That night there was no fire.

The large fire that had cooked the meal and warmed the bones of the weary group of travelers was nothing more than a smoldering pile of coals when the storyteller finished speaking that evening. Neither the boy nor the old man bothered to reach for additional kindling during the telling of the story. The others had gone to sleep hours previously.

"My son," the storyteller said, "I've told much of the story this evening; and yet, there's still much to tell. I can see there's something on your mind. Speak."

"I didn't want to interrupt. But there were things I didn't understand."

"Yes, my son."

"You said the boy was like an elephant or a young steer."

"Oh yes," the storyteller replied, "you wouldn't know of these. Ancient beasts they were, now long extinct. The

elephant was a massive creature. He was the height of three men and the length of six. He walked on all four legs. He had razor sharp tusks the length of a boy and could split a man in two. In front of him was a long trunk. It was a snakelike appendage that he used to squeeze the life out of his prey."

The boy tucked his knees up to his chest.

"The steer," the storyteller continued, "was not so big as his cousin the elephant."

"They were cousins?"

"Of course. He was as tall as a man and twice as long. He walked on all four legs and the horns on his head were as long as your arm. The beast had a temper too. If a man just looked at him wrong, he'd charge him and smash him with the bone of his skull, and gore him with the points of his horns."

The boy stared up at the storyteller frightened.

"Oh," the storyteller said, "but you don't have to worry about those beasts anymore. The ancient beasts have all vanished from the world. There was a time when man had tamed the ancient steer. Our people would eat of his flesh. But those days are gone now."

"It must have been dangerous," the boy said.

The old storyteller shook his head. "No, my son, man was in no danger from the steer that he dominated. The steer was a big animal. It fed many. The danger is in there not being enough. If we don't capture the rabbit, if we don't harvest the grasshopper, if we don't find the fruit, if we don't net the fish, we starve. The ancient man grew his food in a fence and never worried that he wouldn't find it."

The boy nodded his head. "But Iniko was not like a steer. He was not like the elephant then."

"Iniko," the storyteller said, "was like a young steer, a young elephant. When young, those beasts were as helpless as a boy."

The boy nodded his head.

"Well, my son," the storyteller said, "I must rest. We continue our story tomorrow."

CHAPTER V

That night the storyteller woke from a nightmare. The same dream had haunted his nights since he was a young man. It first appeared only in glimpses. He would wake from the nightmare and only remember fragmented moments in time. Then it came to him as a full vision during a time of great difficulty. It was late in the day when the vision appeared, and he had not eaten for a week. In it, he could feel the presence of an inescapable force. His whole frame was gripped with fear.

There were concrete objects in the vision as well. He could see a young boy murdered. The murdered boy awoke. "you have no son," the boy said. In the vision and in the dream, he always said that. A spirit floats out of the dead boy's body. "Disinherited," it would say as it floated upward towards oblivion.

The boy, now spiritless, turned his head in an unnatural direction. His skin was ashen grey. He was naked. From the wound of a dagger, black blood flowed. "He shall

NOT," the boy said "come forth out of thine own bowels who shall be thine heir."

On most nights the dream ended here, but the original vision had more. The dream the storyteller had that night, was much like the original vision. In the dream, the boy stood up. Behind him, a field of dead flowers, each flower six feet tall swayed with a wind that the storyteller could not feel. "Count the number of these dead stalks," *the boy said,* "if thou be able to number them, so shall thy seed be."

The storyteller believed in the boy. He counted on him for his treachery. From amongst the flowers, a heifer, a female goat, a ram, a turtledove, and a pigeon appeared. Each had its throat slit. Black blood flowed. Carrion pecked at the dead. And the storyteller did nothing.

He turned back towards the boy. "This land shall thee inherit," *the boy said with his arm pointing out towards a vast, untamed wilderness.* "Know of a surety," *the boy continued,* "that thy seed shall be a stranger in a land that is not theirs, and shall be hunted by them, killed by them, be afflicted by them four hundred years." *At this, the storyteller always felt horror and great darkness.* "And after," *the boy said.* "When that nation should fall, when the men that hunted thee shall depart from this world, thy seed will inherit the fruitless void, and chaos will reign."

The wound on the boy's chest suddenly healed. His skin colored peach. His lips were red. His eyes disappeared into the blackness of hollow sockets, yet the storyteller always felt that the boy could still see.

When he felt particularly brave, as he had during the dream this night, the storyteller walked up to the boy and stared into the empty eye sockets. The boy leaned his head back. From above him, the storyteller stared directly into the sockets. Within the shell of the skin, there is only nothingness, and nothing else. And then, the eyes became mirrors, and the storyteller saw his self.

The storyteller was afraid of this nightmare, but from it he did not despair. The dream appeared to him as a threat not as inevitability. He saw it as a manifestation of his greatest fears during a time of terrible desolation, not as the words from an immutable power outside of himself. There were times when he thought he saw this vision before him. He thought he saw the dream in the people around him. There was one time, long ago, that he lived it not knowing until it was too late.

He closed his eyes, but he did not sleep.

In the morning, the group packed up camp and left. The storyteller walked with the boy. When night finally came, he continued his story.

In the morning, the family packed up camp and walked out towards the highway. Abraham searched the northbound stretch of road with the scope from his rail gun. He saw nothing.

Iniko walked beside his mother throughout the morning. Abraham walked behind. Everyone was tired; everyone was sore, and the family moved slower than the day before. The weight of the packs had also been redistributed.

Abraham carried more of the weight. Iniko carried less.

Lunch was eaten in the same manner that it had been eaten the day before. One thing was different. The meal was not followed by any silliness whatsoever.

In the afternoon Iniko walked beside his mother. Abraham walked behind. The packs were lighter. There was less water in each. With his thumbs, Abraham readjusted his pack straps every few steps. Iniko stopped every so often to arch his back. Whenever Iniko stopped, Sarah put a hand on his shoulder and smiled gravely.

On this day, not much conversation was had. The plains stretched before them. The mountains were not yet in sight.

At night they camped with no fire. In the morning, the family packed up camp and walked out towards the highway. Abraham searched the northbound stretch of road with the scope from his rail gun. He saw nothing. The packs were very light on this day.

Late in the morning Abraham said to Sarah, "We'll want water soon."

"Is there any to be had?" Sarah questioned.

"Here?" Abraham said condescendingly.

After this, Abraham and his family continued in silence. The packs were much lighter now, too light.

"There's enough for another day," Sarah said, "If we're mindful."

"All we need is a puddle. With this filter," Abraham said, "that's all we need."

"We'll find something," Iniko said hopefully.

Beyond the hazy mirage that rose from the end of the road, the mountains were coming into view.

"We will," Sarah said.

Abraham said nothing. He looked to his left and saw the barren plains. He looked to his right and saw the same. Ahead though, ahead were the mountains and above the mountains, storm clouds could be seen.

The sun was at the top of the sky when the family turned off the road to eat the afternoon meal. Underneath the shelter of low, bushy trees, Abraham put down his pack and sat in the dirt. Sarah and Iniko put down their packs leaning against the cushion of packed clothing and empty water containers.

Abraham held up a clear bottle. It was half full. "We should finish this and save the rest for tonight."

Sarah nodded her head. She pulled out three meal bars, smiled, and said, "at least we'll never run out of these."

Iniko laughed. Abraham did too, but only Sarah could tell he was manufacturing it.

The car had been filled high with food and water when the family departed from the city. The packs could not carry it all. Each pack had a limit that could not be surpassed. Each pack would inevitably run out.

Abraham hoped to reach Church Peak. The old hotel would have stockpiles of canned goods he reasoned. But even stockpiles have a narrowly defined limit. A man must eat to live; men must eat to live; there is a minimum he and them must eat. Even large amounts will diminish when the want exceeds the mass of the whole.

With a dry mouth, Abraham labored with his meal bar. Each swallow felt like a chore. He watched as Iniko took a deep swallow of water from the bottle. He handed the bottle to Sarah, who took a swallow, and said to Abraham "finish it." He took the bottle in his shaking left hand and raised it to his cracked lips. He took a small sip and handed it to Iniko.

"I'm not thirsty," he said smiling.

Iniko turned his head towards his mother who looked back at him uneasily. He extended the water bottle back towards his father who sat staring out into the barren wilderness of the plains. Iniko held the water bottle extended, but Abraham would not take it from his hand.

Sarah sighed. "It's ok," she said to her son, "he wants you to have it."

Iniko hesitated a moment more, staring into the bright blue eyes of the gaunt figure. He hesitated and then shrugged his shoulders. He drank the rest and capped the bottle.

Each day the family did half of the walking before this afternoon meal and the other half after the meal. It was late in the day, right before the time when the family would normally begin searching for a place to camp when Sarah, who had been staring at the ground, gazed out into the open space and saw something that she had not expected to see.

"That's not a mirage," Abraham said. He readjusted the weight of the rail gun. The strap went over his left shoulder and under his right arm. He carried it in front of him. "It's water, but it'll take half a day to get to it. We'll still have to conserve tonight, but not so frugally as we did this afternoon."

Sarah let out a deep sigh. She smiled at Iniko who had overheard the conversation. "See, I knew we'd find something."

Abraham put a hand on his shoulder. "We'll have to be careful," he said to Sarah. He readjusted the weight of the rail gun. "Really careful. It's a reservoir. That's an old farm up there. Not a factory farm. Real people lived there and worked there. I remember from when we visited years ago. We stopped at a roadside stand. Remember that?"

"I remember," Sarah answered, "I remember what I said to you when we saw it. I said, 'you really trust a tomato that was grown on the side of the road.'"

Abraham smiled, "I remember. I couldn't believe real people lived out here, living with the crops. It just isn't done that way. Well, anyway, from what I've heard, farms up here've been abandoned since the occupation."

"With your filter, it could be a filthy puddle and it wouldn't hurt us."

Abraham smiled at his son's innocence. "The water's fine

my boy," Abraham said, "I'm worried about what lurks beneath and what we might find hiding on the banks."

"Oh," Iniko replied feeling embarrassed.

"Don't be afraid," Abraham said, "we'll be cautious. For all I know, the farm is still abandoned."

The next day, Abraham led his family towards the reservoir and the abandoned farm. No-one spoke throughout the morning. As the family approached, a large barn came into view. The bright red siding could be seen from a very long distance on the open plains. A long white fence stretched the length of the highway.

A farmhouse stood beyond the barn. The reservoir was beyond the farmhouse.

Inside of the fence the fields were indistinguishable. What had grown here, no man could tell. A random assortment of grasses, all native to the area, grew wildly, where crops had been tamed before.

Abraham studied the barn. He studied the old farmhouse. He saw no movement, yet he felt warmth in each of the buildings. He could not quite discern its source. But neither felt abandoned.

He pushed this feeling aside and trudged on. He gripped his rail gun with both hands.

The water that Sarah and Iniko had packed was now gone. It would take another day before the family reached the gradual incline of the mountains, and even then there was no promise that water would be found. This reservoir was likely to be the only water that the family would find for several days. Without this water, it was unlikely that Abraham and his family would finish the trek to Church Peak.

The reservoir was very close when Abraham's nervous thoughts were interrupted by the voice of Sarah, "What's that?" was all she said.

In the road, there was a strange object. It was still too far away to tell what it was. As Abraham got closer, he began to perceive its significance. The object was yellow. It was a cylinder. The top of it reflected the light of the sun.

Abraham picked it up. "Creamed Corn," he read out loud. He turned the can over and checked the expiration date. "Still has another couple years," he said. He looked inside the hollow can. "Scraped clean," he said noticing that the paper wrapper was still attached to the can. It hadn't been rained on. The paper was not discolored at all.

From the can he turned his head towards the farmhouse. He looked back at the can and then dropped it on the ground. He shouldered his rail gun.

"Sarah," he said, "that can's only been here a day or two. I'd bet there's more from where it came from." He said this pointing the rail gun towards the farmhouse.

"I think we have enough food," Sarah said reproachfully.

"We do," Abraham replied, "and this isn't where I'd try

getting more. That's not what I'm saying. This farm is not abandoned."

Sarah shouldered her rail gun. "Iniko," she said. "Take out your revolver. Make sure the safety is on. You know how to use it. Just have it out in case you need it."

Iniko's hand shook as he took out the revolver.

Out in the distance Abraham was able to hear a sharp creaking sound. He could hear it, and a moment later he could feel a mild breeze coming from the direction of the old farmhouse. He brought the scope up to his right eye.

Again he heard the sharp squeak. Looking through the scope he could see an old, wooden screen door. As the breeze blew through the wide, open porch it caught the bottom of the door. Abraham watched the screen door and saw nothing else.

With the aid of his scope, Abraham studied the other external features of the house. The porch was held up by five pillars. These were covered in white vinyl and one was broken. The pickets were also very white.

The porch was under shadow. Two windows were just visible on either side of the door. The door had a window itself. The window appeared broken. White vinyl lattice covered the space below the porch. The lattice wrapped around the underside of the entire porch. Beneath was shadow.

He pulled the scope up towards the second floor of the house. Bright blue vinyl siding surrounded four darkened windows. The roof was covered in light brown shingles. Abraham noticed a dark black space where a shingle had become detached.

"It seems abandoned," Sarah said.

"It's certainly meant to seem that way," Abraham replied. "Do you see that?"

"No, what?" Sarah replied.

Abraham lowered his rail gun and pointed towards the stone walkway that led to the porch. "The grass is growing through the stones. But then, look there." Abraham pointed just behind the house. "That trail through the grass leads to back of the house."

"I wouldn't have noticed." Sarah responded. After a few moments she said, "Who are they hiding from?"

"I doubt from us. Keep that gun up," Abraham said. "We can't go without water."

Abraham began walking down the road. "We'll just walk past the house and help ourselves to the reservoir. Then we'll be on our way."

He took a few steps and said, "Just stay calm. We're not here to cause trouble. Walk confidently. Let them see you're carrying something."

Abraham continued walking with Sarah next to him, both shouldering rail guns, and Iniko behind, the revolver shaky in his hands. The screen door creaked again and Iniko turned his head towards the farmhouse in horror. "Just the wind," Abraham said. "Don't worry my boy, it's just the wind."

"How do you know?" Iniko stammered.

Abraham was taken aback. "I watched it. I know."

"How do you know it's empty?"

"That's not where they'd be," Abraham answered.

The sun was hot and at the top of the sky. Normally, local farmers would be working night and day bringing in the harvest this time of year.

In the distance a low hill stood at the edge of the fields. From the road the fields appeared overgrown. But from the road only some of the fields were in view. Beyond that low hill the fields continued. Beyond that low hill the eye could not see.

Abraham kept his eyes away from that low hill. He kept his eyes away from the subtle contour of the trail that wound from the back of the farmhouse to the back of the low hill. Abraham kept his eyes forward to the road and the reservoir, for the water was needed regardless of danger.

"We're half way there. Just keep calm my boy."

"We're past the house," Iniko said.

"Keep your eyes on the reservoir," Sarah said, "and you'll never have to look back at the old farmhouse again."

Abraham kept his eyes on the reservoir. From this distance,

the pool appeared as a sheet of glass reflecting the low hill that stood in the distance. The hill appeared in reverse with the land at the top of the reflection and the sky below. In the center, a single ripple did not interfere with the perfect image in the glass. At the edges however, the mild breeze sent rolling peals of water towards the shoreline. It was just at the edges that the pool seemed a pool. Tall grasses surrounded the edge. A thin trail, barely noticeable ran from the hill behind. In the reflection, no trail could be seen.

Abraham and his family approached. He was within feet when his reflection materialized in the glassy surface of the reservoir. Sarah stood to his right, Iniko to his left. He took a step closer, and his figure began to shift with the ripples at the edge of the reservoir.

Abraham put his pack down and noticed that Iniko was trembling. "Put your pack down son," Abraham said. Holding his rail gun at his shoulder, Abraham scanned the horizon.

Sarah put down hers and began rummaging through the extra garments to find the water filter. Her hands shook. She pulled it out without saying a word. She was still shaking when she assembled the input tube. The output had no tube. It connected directly to the bottles.

Sarah kneeled down beside the edge of the reservoir that was shifting only slightly. She lowered the input tube into the water. "Your bottle," she said to Iniko.

With the bottle attached, Sarah began pumping the handle.

Her hands still shook as the water filled the bottle in short spurts.

The bottle was half full. Sarah's arm, which was fatigued already, had grown tight and was tiring. She stopped for a moment. Only halfway through the first bottle, she turned her head up towards Abraham with eyes of concern.

"I'll do the pumping," Abraham said.

His gun, he put it down.

Sarah stood up and handed him the filter.

She turned around towards her rail gun.

"Leave that on the ground," was what the family heard yelled from the tall grass as Sarah reached for the rail gun.

"Leave it," was yelled and Sarah recoiled backwards as she heard the sound of a gunshot.

"Leave it right there."

Abraham held the filter down at his side.

"We're walking out towards you," the voice said. "Stay right there. We won't harm you. Stay right there."

Five figures emerged from the tall grass beside the bank of the reservoir. Abraham stared into the reflection. He saw the hill. He saw the sky below. He saw his form moving with the gentle sway of the ripples near the edge. He saw the five figures that had been there all along, hidden amongst the reeds, but always in the picture.

"What do they want?" Sarah whispered.

In the same moment, Abraham could see that Iniko was still carrying the revolver. "Put it down," he said to Iniko harsher than he intended. "Not us," he whispered hurriedly, unconvincingly back to Sarah.

"That's all for tonight," the storyteller said to the boy whose tired eyes stared intently across the fire.

The boy did not argue. "What'll happen?" he asked the old man.

"Tomorrow night my son," the old storyteller answered, "tomorrow night." He stretched out beside the fire and closed his eyes.

CHAPTER VI

In the morning the group did not break camp. Instead, the fire was refueled. The young men went out for more wood. The older men set traps and carried nets down to the river.

The women awoke later in the morning. They woke, gathered together, and began carrying water containers down the steep slope of the hill.

When the boy had finished gathering firewood with the others, he walked down towards the river to find that the storyteller, along with four other men, was carrying a giant catfish.

The women, smiling and carrying water bottles, walked past the men with the fish.

That night a feast was had. Around the fire, the forms of the men and women of the group moved to self-made rhythms. The revelry went late into the night and when it was over, the storyteller found the boy sitting alone. He sat beside him away from the fire, for that night it was hot.

"Two more nights after this night and then we make the final push up the mountain," the storyteller said to the boy with his hand on his back.

The boy, with his knees tucked-in replied, "Have you done this every year? Is it true? Are there really thousands?"

"Just like us my son," the storyteller replied. "Thousands just like us who trap and fish and look after each other. I was one of the first of our lot to make the pilgrimage, and I have been in attendance every year since."

"I feel weird about it," the boy replied. "My first group, they weren't like you. I feel shame from it."

"Neither was mine," the storyteller replied with sadness in his crystal blue eyes. "At one time, we all lived that way."

The boy turned his head up towards the old storyteller and un-tucked his knees. "Will you tell me the story now?" he asked.

Unbeknownst to them, Abraham's family had ventured into the Vale of Siddim. Several private farms filled the valley; the farms were well stocked with preserved foods. The pantries were still stocked in spite of the year that had elapsed since operations had ceased.

Men from the old nation were not permitted to live here, yet hidden in the valley; farmers grew crops and hunted the animals. The invaders could not prevent it. The flying machines had limitations. Men, well hidden could remain undetected by the vision of aerial drones. It was not until many years later that all was destroyed, years later when the robotic men were sent into the countryside.

Abraham, when the men sprung out from hiding, was not at all surprised. His anger though, his anger for a moment was fierce. He did not show it. But it filled his arms and legs; it filled his chest; he felt it red hot in his cheeks.

He had known. His thirst, the eyes of his son, Sarah, all distracted him from an all too apparent truth. This was not water to be had.

"Hands up in the air," the voice said and a body came into focus, "keep your hands away from those side arms."

The hands of Abraham and Sarah lifted. Iniko's did too.

"Bera," the voice said, "walk up and take the side arms. And do it polite. No getting fresh you damn sodomite."

Bera walked up to Abraham. He smelled of putrid flesh and the sludge that forms at the edge of a stagnant puddle. His bony, blackened fingers reached for the grip of Sarah's pistol. He grinned up at her and chortled inwardly.

He reached next for Abraham who turned his head away when the smell of the creature's greasy black hair wafted by his nose.

Holding the two handguns, Bera skulked back towards the other four men. He had a slight hunch, and he carried his shoulders oddly close to his ears.

"You missed one," Abraham said. "It's on the ground next to my son."

Bera jerked around, his long arms rotating around his body freely with the pistols still in his hands. The thin arms, with the weight of the handguns on the ends, flopped loosely around the oddly shaped torso that was unnaturally thin in the chest yet inflated out of proportion in the gut.

He did not say a word. He chortled inwardly and walked back over to the family. He reached down next to Iniko, who was too afraid to notice the stench, and retrieved the ancient revolver.

"You have now met Bera," the voice said, the same voice that came from the tall grass, "You'll call me Birsha. These are Shinab, Shem, and Zoar."

"It's a pleasure," Abraham said with a wry grin. "We only wanted water, nothing else. There is no need for introductions. We will be on our way soon enough."

"Not from there," Birsha replied.

At this, the fists of Abraham tightened.

"Not from there," Birsha replied. "No, you won't want that."

"Our filter," Abraham began but was interrupted.

"Yep," Shem said cutting him off, "that won't do much for it. Not if it were the best ever made. A year ago," he began but stopped, seeming to be lost in thought.

"A year ago," Shinab continued for Shem, "invaders came and poisoned it."

At this, all five men lowered their automatic rifles.

"We mean you no harm," Birsha said. "Hell, if we had let you alone, that young boy of yours would be gone by now."

"How do you know," Abraham said. His mouth was dry.

"Give her a taste," said Zoar. Bera chortled.

Abraham did not laugh.

"It's salty," Birsha said. "A taste won't kill you, but a mouthful. A mouthful is all it takes," he said stammering. He peered off into the distance, "That filter won't do anything for it. We'd tried that early on."

"Mouthful of salt water," Sarah said questioningly.

"It's not salt," Birsha said, "just tastes like it is."

Abraham gazed down towards Iniko and then back up towards Birsha. The man's thick hair was matted on his head. It was mostly grey, with layers of dark brown hidden beneath. He stood always to one side with the left shoulder higher than the right. This wasn't a disfigurement. He was certainly not born with a slouch. He just stood with one. He carried the automatic rifle carelessly with his right hand and peered through his left eye.

Birsha spit. The leftover trail of mucous coated his lower lip. With his hairy left forearm, he wiped it.

Shem and Shinab, the two men standing on either side of Birsha, were not entirely amorphous. Both pudgy with swollen faces, these creatures seemed more like pigs than humans. Pink skin, large buck teeth, hairless arms and legs, squinting eyes, fat guts, were present in both of these men who were surprisingly unrelated. The single physical discrepancy in their appearance was found on the side of Shem's head. A scar, a raised crescent beginning a fingers length behind his right eye and up towards the crown of his skull marked a significant difference between himself and Shinab.

Shinab was there on the day that the scar was made. He watched his companion closely ever since. He was doing this on the day that Abraham met him. Every few seconds, Shinab turned his head towards his companion.

"Salty, Salty, Salty, Salty," Bera suddenly screamed with his head tilted back towards the sky. "Salty, Salty."

"Don't let it bother you," Zoar said. "He does that. Nervous habit. That sorta thing."

When he said this, Zoar had been standing away from the other four men. Long black hair fell loosely down towards his shoulders. His eyes were dark. His beard was thick. He still had his finger on the trigger of his automatic rifle. It was pointed towards the ground.

"Salty," Bera said. This time he said it quietly.

"Why salty?" Sarah asked.

"Ain't like that," Zoar replied, "Naw, ain't like that. Any word'll do for him. Usually ain't no word at 'all. Some nights, he be standing, right out there, naked as hell screamin off that head of his. No harm in it. Won't bother you."

Sarah shook her head in confusion.

Abraham parted his cracked lips and asked, "If you mean us no harm, can we have our guns back? We would like to be on our way."

"If we give the guns back," Birsha replied, "how do we know that you won't come back in the middle of the night. How do we know that you don't intend to come back and rob us?"

Bera chortled.

Abraham smirked and his eyes fell to the ground.

"Besides," Birsha replied, "you seem as if you could use some water. We can part with water. We have a spring. You can stay for three days, but when you leave, those guns are staying here."

Abraham silenced Sarah's anger before its voice could be heard. It took only a glance.

"Ok," he said. "That's more than fair. We are in need of a safe place to rest. We are in need of food and water."

"You'll have that here," Shinab said. "You'll have that here."

"As you might imagine," Birsha said, "under the circumstances, it is necessary that we confine you."

Abraham shook his head. "Under the circumstances that seems fair."

Bera, now carrying a length of rope, walked over to Abraham. He bound his hands.

Abraham watched as he did the same to Sarah and then to Iniko.

Sarah did not let her anger show. Even as the rope was stretched around the wrists of her son's arms, she showed nothing.

"When you are ready to depart," Birsha said with his left eye closed entirely, and a clever grimace filling the lower half of his face, "just say so and your bounds will be cut."

Sarah said nothing.

"You'll be our house guests," Birsha said, his grimace transparently mischievous, "some doors will be locked, barring your admittance, but the front door will always remain open. Stay for as long as three days. Or leave tonight. It makes no difference to us."

"We'll take the full invitation," Abraham said, masking his recognition of Birsha's smile with a façade of appreciation.

"Allow me to lead the way," Birsha said. "We're the kings of the vale. That's what we call ourselves. The five kings of the vale." He began to walk towards the house but then stopped lazily. "Shem, Shinab," he said, "grab their bags. I hope you don't mind us having a peek before we return them to you."

"Not at all," Abraham replied. He did not introduce himself or his family. His name was not asked for.

Birsha turned back towards the house striding unevenly. Sarah and Iniko followed first.

Abraham walked behind his son feeling the shifting weight of the knife in his right cargo pocket with every step of his right foot.

The trail that led from the reservoir to the back of the house was surprisingly wide. From a distance it was invisible, but up close it was equal in width to the length of a man's leg. The trail led up to a cellar door. The door was on the ground and the red paint of its surface was chipped and bubbled.

Bera swung the door open with an awkward yank from his shoulder up towards the sky. The additional flourish, the extra effort caused the door to swing open wildly. The handle struck the ground and the entire door bounced. He opened the second door and screamed something that was altogether unintelligible, staring at the sky above him, his arms out to his sides, his hollow chest fully exposed.

Birsha walked past Bera and climbed down the stairs leading Abraham and his family into the basement of the house.

"Never use the front door," Birsha said as the family reached the cold damp of the concrete floor. A single light lit the stone cellar walls. Shadows climbed out behind the stockpiles of canned goods. Produce too was packed neatly in bins. It was not at all what Abraham had expected. It was cold and dark, but the meticulous organization of food supplies did not at all match the shabby appearance of the men responsible.

"You said that we could..." Sarah had begun to say but was cut off.

"An expression, " Birsha replied, "I beg your pardon. You may never use the front door. But you can leave through the back anytime you wish."

Birsha noticed that Abraham was eying the sacks of potatoes that sat in the corner across from the cellar entrance.

"We're very well stocked," Birsha said suddenly. "This is after all, our livelihood. The world as it was known to us may have ended, but we will continue. We will survive because of this." He turned around in a circle with his arms held out in front of him. A moment later Bera stumbled down the steps. The other three men had already made it down.

Bera stumbled down and fell catching himself with the palms of his hands. The side of his face struck the concrete rather harshly. With loud sobs, Bera began to cry. He picked himself up enough so that he could sit in the middle of the cellar floor. He cried like a young child. His face, the part that had struck the concrete, was in his hands. The tears fell down the hideous face. Spots formed on the ground between his legs.

He was there only a moment when Birsha rushed towards him. Birsha put his arm around the sobbing creature. He rubbed his back. His hand slid up and down. His hand slid from the top of the shoulder blades down to the lowest part of the lower back and up again. Up and down, up and down the hand slid.

Bera was not yet calm when Zoar led Abraham and his family up the stairs into a darkened living room. The stairs to the rooms above were to the right. Abraham turned to the left and found two couches covered in old brown blankets. The couches were the color of dirt. The windows let in very little light. The panes had been painted black.

Abraham stepped towards the couch whose back was fully exposed. Flies buzzed. A long creak came from the floor boards below. He took another step and felt the weight of the knife rub against his outer thigh.

The walls were not blank. An old portrait, a family portrait in a decorative frame rested above the fireplace beyond the exposed back of the couch. A big dark man stood tall with a young light woman. A Brown child was at their feet. The picture was taken in front of a tree.

Abraham walked past the couch. The family in the portrait stared into his heart. The white wife smiled coyly. Her husband's eyes were deep. The little girl appeared to be giggling. But something was amiss. Dirt had stained the surface of the painting. Her dress, which must have been clean at the time of the photo, was a dark red-brown in a single curious place. The left side of her chest was coated in red-brown.

With his finger, Abraham rubbed the stain. The dirt had

caked.

He stepped back. In the photo, a solitary ram could be seen standing behind a bush. His coat was clean. Above the family there was nothing. The color was faded, but it must have been blue. No clouds could be seen, nothing was above.

Sarah grabbed his arm with both her hands and Abraham started.

"Come on," she said. Zoar said that he'd show us up. They have a room for us."

"Yea," Zoar said, "Up this way. Come on up. This's where you stayin."

The room upstairs was at the end of the hallway. The room's window faced out towards the highway. Abraham could not see by looking out. The window was painted black. He assumed it faced the road because it took a left turn to reach it.

"Make yerselfs comfortable." Zoar said.

Sarah and Iniko walked into the center of the room. Abraham licked his lips. "Water," he asked.

Zoar nodded his head. "Yea, I guess you folks must be pretty dry. Come on down and we'll fetch ya some."

Sarah did not move. Iniko tried to put his arms around her. He grabbed at her desperately with his bound hands. She tousled his hair with affection, not playfulness. She lifted her bound hands above his head and around his shoulders pulling him towards her.

"I will come down," Abraham said. "It has been a long day."

"Suit yerself."

Zoar walked out of the room.

Abraham took Sarah into his arms and kissed her deeply.

"I'll be right back up," he said, "we'll have some water and we'll talk."

Sarah trembled as he walked out of the bedroom door, the weight of the knife shifting in his right cargo pocket with every other step.

She ushered Iniko to the mattress that lay in the far corner of the room. With her son she sat down holding his head on her breast. Tears streamed down his cheeks. She felt the warmth soak into her shirt. She smelt his sweat, and the days he had gone without a shower. Above all, she smelt his fear.

Sound did not travel easily through this old house. Sarah could not have heard what had happened below. A look of surprise filled her face when Abraham returned to the frame of the bedroom door; his hands clean, supporting the weight of a jug. Iniko was in her arms. Her shirt was wet.

Iniko appeared relieved.

Abraham crossed the room towards the mattress in three heavy steps. He put the jug down in front of Sarah and sat down awkwardly with his hands bound on the floor next to his wife.

Abraham took a long pull on the jug and handed it to Sarah. She drank with both hands and handed the jug to Iniko. The jug went around four times before Sarah began to speak.

"What could they want?" she asked.

Abraham shook his head. "They're not like the deserters," he answered, "I don't think they're like the deserters."

Sarah wanted to say that she was afraid. She turned towards Iniko and said nothing.

Abraham said, "Whatever their purpose is, it is not generosity. Just look at them. No, they want something from us. I just can't tell what it is."

"Maybe they want guns," Sarah said.

"They have guns. They have our guns. Why keep us here? Why tie our hands? Why didn't they just shoot us?"

Sarah considered for a moment and answered, "Maybe they are decent people. Maybe they aren't murderers."

"They murdered the former owners of this house," Abraham said. "Look at them. To kill someone, to smile at someone, to them there is no difference. In my entire life, I have never seen people so wretched as these."

Iniko began to cry.

"Then what do they want?" Sarah said.

"What could they possibly want?" Abraham repeated. "They should have killed us. Why does he want us here for three days?"

Sarah shook her head. "Your knife?" she asked.

"I have it. But I am no murderer. These men have given us water. They have promised us food and shelter for three nights. It was different with the guards on the bridge. They would have certainly killed us. It was different with Farrow and the deserters. They meant us harm. They meant to rape you. It was different with Adam and Evelyn. They meant to steal from us."

Sarah rested her chin on the palm of her hand. "Our guns. Is that not enough?"

"We'll have them back," Abraham replied. "We will say that our intention is to stay all three nights. But on the second night we will leave, for if there is any ill-intention, it is to be on that third night. Sound does not carry through this house. There is a board that squeaks next to the stairs. But everywhere else, silence can be had. When everyone is asleep tonight, I will find our guns. I'll find our bags. Tomorrow night we depart."

Sarah smiled gravely. This response from Abraham, she had not expected.

Iniko stopped crying. He smiled at his father.

"It won't be long," the storyteller said, "before the sun peaks out over the horizon."

"I'm not tired," the boy said.

"Good night my son," the old storyteller said as he laid back and fell asleep.

CHAPTER VII

The storyteller had never met this man in his life. He met him only in this nightmare. Over and over, he had felt this same introduction since his night of great misfortune. Over and over within the horrorscape of a deep red background from behind a dead cypress, the man, his head detached, speaking through the space in his roughly cut neck, said "Abram, it is me, have you forgotten. Abram your brother Lot. It is me."

The body of the man staggered. It was naked and without genitalia. There was no scar. It seemed as if there had never been anything there. The storyteller, when noticing this in the nightmare, felt a strong emotion pass over him. He felt as if this creature had been deprived of some sacred rite.

The creature as a whole appeared as a holograph would. The image fluttered like a dry, dead leaf flutters in the wind.

"Left to die," the image said. "Left to die. I asked for nothing more than a shoelatchet. Mine had been taken. Chedorlaomer. Left to die."

At this, the storyteller awoke. The sun had risen, but the fog was thick. "I keep only the brother who keeps me," he mumbled to himself. He said this not as an excuse for a wrong, but as a truth found in a world ruled once again by the state of nature.

Later that day he found the boy crouched behind a tree. He was hiding. The storyteller's sudden appearance shocked him. The boy hid something behind his back.

"And what's this?" the storyteller asked.

The boy was ashamed.

"Have out with it," the storyteller commanded.

In his hand the boy held a piece of smoked catfish.

"This is not meal time," the storyteller said. "And that was from the common larder."

The boy began to cry.

The storyteller reached out his hand in which the boy placed the piece of smoked catfish.

"Did you learn nothing from the story?" the storyteller asked. "Did you learn nothing?"

The boy continued to cry.

"Thou shalt not steal," the storyteller said. "Would you be

as Adam Lot? Would you sacrifice your life for the theft of another's morsel? Would you be as Evelyn? Would you walk naked before the world too proud to hide your evil?"

"I'm sorry," escaped the lips of the boy.

"Sorry," the storyteller said, "you tell me that you are sorry. You spit in the face of your people. You spit in the face of the people who have taken you in and say you are sorry. Every night I tell you our story and you listen with excitement, but you hear nothing. This is our story. This is what makes us who we are. This is what separates us from the degraded beasts that prey on the weak. This is why we survive when all others have been folded into the dust of the ground. This is why we make this pilgrimage. To remember who we are."

"I'm sorry."

"Tonight you tell the whole group. Tonight you tell all of your sin. Only then will you be forgiven."

That night, in front of the whole group, the boy stood naked and confessed his sin.

As he confessed, the faces of the people were blank. When he was finished, one at a time, the people came forward and embraced him with compassion in their eyes. The storyteller was last. He held the boy for a moment.

"Put your clothes on and come away with me," the storyteller said, "there is still much of the story to be told."

Walking with the boy, the storyteller continued his tale.

That night Abraham and his family were invited to join the five kings for dinner. As Abraham walked down the stairs he heard voices coming from the other side of the house. He walked through the living room into a dark hallway. At the time, Abraham could not figure the reason, but something about this hallway made it seem as an illusion. Perhaps it was the lack of light or the dark green paint. Something gave the hallway an appearance of longevity. Something gave the hallway the appearance of false hope.

The walls were covered in family pictures. The father, the mother, and the daughter from the family portrait were in most of the photos that hung on the wall. There were others too, but these did not come to Abraham's notice. He was particularly intrigued by a single photo. It was a photo taken of the daughter. He was surprised to find that the daughter in this picture was grown up. Her mother and father were in this photo too. Each was smiling. All were happy.

Abraham smiled to himself and turned away from the picture to look down the hallway of false hope. Sarah and Iniko were next to him; each was smiling.

The dining room was across from the kitchen. The door to the dining room was wide open. The kitchen door was locked.

Abraham turned into the dimly lit dining room surprised to find that it was meticulously kept. Candles burned in three corners of the room. A lamp hung from the ceiling with a large candle in the center. The entire house was a trash heap, but the basement and the dining room were kept clean.

On the table seven places were set. White plates, forks, and small sharp knives were placed before each seat. Tall glasses were filled with water, and a jug sat in the center.

Bera was standing in a corner. In a semi-rhythmic fashion he was bobbing up and down. He bent at the waist allowing the line of his upper body to drop perpendicular to his lower half. He then jerked up straight allowing an incomprehensible noise to part from his lips. Up and down, up and down, Bera's face was red from the ceaseless repetition.

Birsha stood up from his seat at the head of the table and ushered Abraham and his family towards the three open seats.

"Water?" Birsha asked politely.

"Yes," Sarah answered.

Birsha poured the contents of the jug into the three empty glasses.

Zoar sat across from Abraham leaning back in his chair with his feet up on the table. His dark eyes remained focused on his glass. He made no effort to acknowledge the presence of the three people who just entered the room.

"Shem and Shinab should be in soon," Birsha said. "They're wonderful cooks."

A moment later the kitchen door swung open. The light from the kitchen was bright. The windows on that side of the house had not been blacked out. Abraham leaned over to catch a glimpse of what lay behind the door. Splotches of red could be seen on the ceiling. He could see nothing beyond this. The pig-like bodies of Shem and Shinab blocked the space below. The door swung closed but opened slightly in the opposite direction on its backswing. On the counters, Abraham could see red. Beyond the counters there was a sliding glass door that opened to a back porch.

The door closed entirely and the two men wearing aprons laid platters on the table. Shinab walked back to the kitchen door holding a key. He put the key in the keyhole at the top of the door and turned it.

"Corn, and…" Shem said pausing for a moment.

"Wild boar," Shinab interjected. "The meat platter is wild boar." He said this with an awkward glance towards Birsha.

Shinab served the guests first. He then served Zoar and Birsha. There was a plate on the floor next to Bera. He threw a piece of meat on it. He served Shem and then himself. The corn and the meat smelled richly of smoke.

Abraham took up the small knife and fork in his hands awkwardly. Glancing up he received a compassionate grin from Birsha.

"I suppose that your bounds are unnecessary," Birsha said. "A precaution that you willingly submitted to. I'm starting to doubt that you mean us any harm. Bera, untie the hands of our guests."

Bera stopped bobbing and walked towards Abraham. He bent over Abraham and untied his hands. Abraham had to turn away. Bera's greasy hair was only a hands length away from his nose. Bera untied Sarah's hands next and then Iniko's.

Sarah's expression, when Bera had finished untying the hands of Iniko, was that of a question. She picked up her utensils and began to eat.

The meal was eaten in silence. Abraham and his family sat at table with four of the five kings. Bera sat in the corner of the room on the floor. He ate with his hands and continued to bob between bites and swallows.

"For over a year," Birsha began when the eating was over, "we have lorded over this Vale. There was very little when our kingships began. The crops would not grow. The roads were teaming with marauders. But in a year, in a year only we have made the land fruitful and destroyed our enemies."

The three kings sitting with Birsha nodded their heads. Bera, from the corner of the room, squealed like a pig.

"Yet," Birsha said and paused, "yet," he continued, "There are four that remain." At this, the kings shook their heads. Bera grunted and farted loudly.

"Amraphel," Birsha hissed, "Arioch… Chedorlaomer… and the Tidal king." Shinab banged his fist on the table. Shem smashed his plate on the floor. Bera farted.

"These kings," Birsha hissed sarcastically, "they mean to take our land. They would have the entire Vale of Siddim to themselves and no-one else. Our castle, our lordships is what they desire. They mean to put our heads on pikes!" Shem stabbed his knife into the table. Zoar, who had not made any displays of anger stared across the table towards Abraham. His eyes were deep and knowing. The stare lasted only a moment.

"Three days hence," Birsha remarked proudly, "in three days we march into the Vale of Siddim to meet our enemies who reside on the opposing side of the reservoir. We will meet them, and we will be victorious!" The four kings at the table stood up and raised their glasses. Bera made a high pitched wining sound.

"Raise your glasses," Birsha boomed, "drink with us friends, Abram, Eshcol, Aner, drink with us." Abraham stood up. Sarah shot him a questioning glance and stood up too, holding Iniko's hand, applying pressure in his palm, the pressure telling her son to rise.

"You have named us," Abraham remarked.

"Your name Abram," Birsha replied, "is many generations older than you. Tonight, your body takes on the name it was given. And three days hence, you and your confederates will ride out and meet the enemy by the sides of Bera, Birsha, Shinab, Shem, and Zoar, rightful kings of the Vale."

"Cheers," Abraham said heartily.

"Cheers," said Sarah. Iniko said nothing. No-one but Abraham noticed his confusion.

"Hurrah," said the four kings, who had been sitting at the table, in hearty, brotherly tones. Bera, still on the floor, bobbed and moaned.

Later that night, when Iniko was fast asleep, Abraham and Sarah spoke in hushed whispers. The couple sat in the infinite darkness of the bedroom.

"Abraham, I'm scared," Sarah said. "At least with the deserters we knew what they wanted. These people," she paused, "these people are insane. They're bat-shit insane. They want us to fight for them? For what? Kings? Seriously, what the hell?"

Abraham nodded his head and through the darkness Sarah could see that he understood. "We'll be gone before the three days are up. We know what they want. They want us to fight for them against their imaginary enemies. That's it. If we leave before the fight, we have nothing to worry about."

"Can you be sure?" Sarah asked. "These people are completely insane. What if they change their minds? And what was with the names? He never asked you what your name was. How did he guess?"

"He pronounced it funny though," Abraham answered, "he called me Abram not Abraham. And I never did give him my name. Maybe it's coincidence and nothing else. The name he gave you was strange enough that I wouldn't think twice about it. But it is weird that he nearly guessed at mine."

Sarah shook her head. "What a bunch of crazy assholes. Seriously, kings? And they smell like shit. And Bera, what the fuck's wrong with that guy acting like a fucking dog?"

Abraham let this pass.

"I want to know what's in that kitchen," Abraham said.

"Why's it locked?" Sarah said sighing.

"I don't know," Abraham replied shaking his head. "I don't know but I saw deep red-black splotches on the ceiling when Shem and Shinab came through the door. There was a pool of red on the counters."

"Blood?" Sarah asked.

"I think so. They must have slaughtered the boar in there. When I walked by after dinner, I noticed that it smelled funny. Even with the door closed there was a smell. It must be used for slaughtering."

Sarah nodded her head. It was dark, but Abraham's eyes were adjusted and he could see this subtle movement.

"There is a glass door at the back of the kitchen," Abraham continued. "It leads to a back porch. That must be where they do their cooking. There must be a fire pit back there. Tomorrow, during the day, I'll try to look through that window. I would like to have a look inside of that kitchen if I can get away with it."

"With all that blood in there," Sarah rejoined, "It would be good to know for sure that the room is used for slaughter and nothing else."

Abraham nodded and stood up. "I think the house is asleep. Wish me luck."

"Be careful," Sarah said.

Abraham pulled off his boots and rolled up the cuffs of his hiking pants. Silently he walked away from Sara towards the frame of the door. Sarah could see his outline as he crossed the threshold into the hallway. She could see him, but she could not hear him, and then he was gone.

Abraham skulked past the first bedroom door on his left. It was closed. He walked up to the second door on the left which was left ajar. The door opened into the bedroom. Abraham could hear a low moaning sound coming from the bedroom. He stopped and listened.

The moan was joined by a high pitch whimper. Abraham crept up to the door and peered inside. A moan, a whimper, a moan, a whimper, the noises came from the voices of two different men. At first, Abraham could not make out the forms that were moving ever so perceptibly in the room.

But then, he recognized Birsha's slumped shoulder. He was standing up thrusting slowly in the direction of the bed. The legs of another man were on his shoulders. Abraham could not see who it was. Then, suddenly, another sound from the lips of the man who was lying on the bed. "Salty, Salty, Salty." And Bera's unique chortling laughter.

Abraham tiptoed away from the door. He let out a sigh of relief, for the fears that he had for his wife's safety had fallen away.

From the bedroom he proceeded towards the stairs. He took each step carefully minding the floor boards. When a board seemed as if it would squeak, he held his weight, lifted his foot and placed it on a different board. He moved slowly but reached the stairs without making a sound. The staircase did not require the same level of precaution. Abraham had noted this earlier that day. At the bottom though, at the landing, Abraham would have to swing his weight around the banister to avoid the large spot that was sure to squeak loudly.

A step away from the landing, and Abraham could hear the snoring of Shem and Shinab. The sounds were nearly identical and came from the two couches in the living room. With both hands Abraham supported his weight on the banister. His left foot remained on the last step of the staircase. On this left foot he pivoted his weight and swung his right foot around the banister avoiding the landing altogether.

He missed the board that he knew would squeak. He landed on a board that squeaked nonetheless. It squeaked under the full force of his right foot landing hard on the board.

The rhythmic sound of the snoring continued, but only from one of the couches. The snoring from the other couch stopped completely.

Abraham was still. He did not breathe. He stood with no motion but that of his heart, which beat vigorously.

Out of the corner of his eye, Abraham could see that the body on the further couch had sat up. It grunted. The head scanned the room. It stared straight at Abraham. It continued to stare.

Then, Abraham heard a deep sigh, then, the sound of that body falling back down into the couch. Abraham still did not move. He did not breathe. His heart beat faster within his chest.

The snore that had gone uninterrupted was finally joined by the rhythm of its companion.

Abraham let out his breath and breathed in deeply. Still, he did not move. He listened to the two couches snoring. He continued to listen until the rhythms were almost identical. He listened and the snores again sounded identical.

Tiptoeing, Abraham skirted around the landing around towards the basement stairs. The stairs did not squeak. He felt the cold concrete under his feet and let out a sigh of relief. He could see his bag in the corner of the room. He opened a zipper and pulled out his flashlight.

He searched the basement with the beam of light. It took only a moment for him to find the place where his guns had been left.

He walked over to the guns. The guns were chained together but the chain appeared weak. The handguns were not secured at all. Abraham picked up a hand gun and checked to see if there was ammunition in the magazine. The bullets were still there. He put down the gun and was about to walk away when he noticed the padlock that was used to connect the two ends of the chain. The key was in it.

Abraham smiled and shook his head in disbelief. "It was all a show," he whispered to himself. "Binding our hands, taking our guns. Birsha, he trusts us now. He wants us to fight with him. He thinks we will fight with him."

Abraham tucked the flashlight into his left cargo pocket to balance out the weight. He was not as careful on his return to the bedroom. He went up both sets of stairs and found that Sarah was still awake. Upon hearing his discoveries, Sarah kissed him. They slept together on a mattress that was laid against the wall adjacent to Iniko. They were quiet. Iniko did not hear them.

In the morning the sun penetrated the blacked out window enough so that the family could see each other in the darkened glow. From the gloom of the bedroom, it seemed bright outside.

Iniko was awake first. Abraham could not have known for sure, but it seemed like Iniko had been awake for some time.

With opened eyes Abraham glanced across the room and looked back at his own naked body. He could feel that he was still inside her. He reached for his pants. He was not sure where his pants had been left. He groped about and found that Sarah was also nude.

Iniko, from the mattress on the other side of the room, looked away.

Abraham stood up, still nude, and saw that his pants were at the foot of the mattress. He stepped into each leg feeling the flashlight in the cargo pocket of the left and the knife in the cargo pocket of the right.

By now, Sarah was awake. Bewildered, she covered her breasts with her arm and reached with her other for her undergarments.

Iniko still looked away.

"How did…" escaped the lips of Sarah. Abraham had no answer. Exhaustion had gotten the better of them was the assumption that each made.

Was it exhaustion though? That was a question that Abraham asked later, years later. Was it exhaustion or was it the house? Was it the Vale of Siddim?

Sarah walked over to her son and embraced him. "Iniko I…"

He recoiled. She let him go.

"While I was in the room," Iniko said and nothing else.

"Give him some space," Abraham said. "It was wrong of us son. I'm sorry."

Iniko breathed out, allowed his shoulders to slump, shook his head dejectedly, and said, "I know. I didn't mean to let you know that I saw. We've been on the move now for days. I don't even know how long."

"I'm sorry Iniko."

"Ok," Iniko replied. "It's ok."

Sarah frowned. There was nothing else she could do.

The family walked down the stairs together. At the bottom of the stairs they were greeted by Zoar. His knowing eyes found Abraham's.

"The others are outside," he said. "Hear Birsha and Bera last night?" he did not wait for a response. "Makes me sick," he said and spit on the floor. "Shem and Shinab are the same. Lock my door at night. Suggest you do the same."

Abraham was taken aback. "Have they tried," he said hesitantly, "with you?"

"No, fuck. Fuck no. But shit if I'd let them dirty sons of bitches try. Hell. Man's gotta take precautions you know."

"Thanks for the advice," Abraham said in earnest.

"We're kings damn it. Kings ought not act that way. Makes a man sick."

Abraham had misunderstood those understanding eyes. It was not disillusionment that Abraham saw last night. It was not a grip on reality that Abraham saw in the eyes of Zoar. It was sodomy, not insanity that disagreed with this man.

"Can see you folks is normal," Zoar said. "That's good if you know what I mean. Shit they do at night just ain't right. Makes a man sick."

"Where are you from?" Sarah asked suddenly.

"United-American by birth ma'am. Just happened to be in the wrong place at the wrong time. You know how it goes, I'm sure."

"Yes we do. How did you end up with these men?"

"Luck just had it that way. I'se on a trip. On vacation. Flights back were canceled. Tried to drive out but got robbed. Lost my identification. Hell, after that. Ain't no way out."

Sarah shook her head.

"Yep, met up with these folks about a year ago. Found this old farm. I'd hate to make you folks uncomfortable but we killed the folks living here. Not much of a choice really. The windows were already blacked out. They was hiding just like we is hiding. Always hiding. But not after tomorrow. Tomorrow we gonna kill them sons of bitches kings from across the reservoir. Birsha figured out the house they was livin in. Birsha figured em out. We're going in the nighttime. Kill em in their beds."

"It sounded like…" Abraham began.

"No, we kill em in their beds. That's the plan. That's what we did here. Birsha just likes to sound pretty."

"He sounded as if he needed us," Abraham said.

Zoar's expression changed suddenly. He looked as if he had said too much. "Well…" he uttered. "I can't say nothing to that. I mean. Yea Birsha thinks we need your help killing em in their beds."

Abraham replied reassuringly, "Of course. We are honored to help."

"Yep. That's what we need you for."

The cellar door could be heard slamming open in the basement below. A strange whine followed. Abraham could not hear the footsteps below. Only sharp, loud noises penetrated the thick air of the house. It was not until the remaining four kings were on the basement steps that he heard anything besides the strange noises escaping from Bera. Abraham made way so that the men could come all the way up the stairs.

"Good morning," Birsha exclaimed. "Breakfast will be served shortly."

Abraham and his family found themselves sitting in the dining room. Canned beans were mixed with canned corn and placed in a large bowl in the center of the table.

"We're unfortunately out of boar," Birsha apologized. "I'm afraid that meat won't be back on the menu until tomorrow night. Until then, we go without." Abraham caught Shinab's hungry eyes as this was said. He picked up his spoon, dipped it into his plate, and took a bite of the cold, canned food.

"How can you be so sure," Sarah asked smiling. "Are you raising pigs?"

"Oh," Birsha said as his face began to redden, "no. I guess we can't be entirely sure. But Shem. He is a talented hunter. When he goes out for boar, he rarely comes back empty handed."

Sarah nodded her head. She was still smiling. "I'm sure he is."

The day was hot. Abraham asked Birsha if he would be permitted to go outside. He was instructed to stay behind the house, to stay on the lawn behind the house and that his wife and child were to stay indoors.

Abraham was not prepared to leave Sarah and Iniko inside without him. He waited most of the day within the confines of the hot upstairs bedroom.

Iniko was no longer mad at him. His forgiveness was so complete that he even let Sarah tousle his hair.

It was late in the day that Abraham heard the cellar door slam open. He walked down the stairs quickly to see if anyone was still in the house.

He found no-one. First he tried the kitchen door. The bolt was locked tight. He went down into the basement. He checked the guns. The key was still in the lock. The cellar door was still open. He climbed the cellar stairs out into the sunshine. At first he felt blinded. His eyes had gotten used to the dim light of the house. After a few moments he was able to see the five figures walking towards the hillside along the trail. The figures moved slowly but in a few moments they vanished entirely.

Abraham ran up to the back porch. He climbed the steps and bounded across the decking. The sun was bright. He had to put his face up to the glass to see into the kitchen. He peered inside and was struck with the horror of the room.

Blood was everywhere. Some was so old that it had blackened entirely. There was a puddle on the floor and above the puddle, a large meat hook hung in the center of the room. Nothing dangled from the hook.

Abraham continued to peer into the kitchen with his hands cupped around the sides of his head. It looked like a slaughter room and nothing else. Ghastly in the way it was kept, but a slaughter room nonetheless. He was about to look away. He was about to turn around when a singular object laying lifelessly in the corner arrested his attention.

Abraham turned his head and nearly threw up. He gagged. He gagged again. He ran towards the steps, past the smoker. He was about to walk down to the cellar but thought to check over his shoulder first. The five figures had not yet emerged. The five were beyond sight. Down in the basement he began talking to himself. "No, I won't tell Sarah. She need not know. Damn, those sick bastards. They fed him to us." He gagged. "I won't tell Sarah. I can't tell Sarah. We're leaving tonight. It makes no difference. He said meat wouldn't be on the menu until tomorrow night."

The old storyteller and the boy were seated beside each other on two large stones. The boy had not remembered how this place was found, for when the story began that evening he was walking by the storyteller's side.

"They're like the others, the poachers," the boy said. "The men who are not like our people."

"Yes," the storyteller said lost in thought. "Yes they were."

"Thieves, murderers, eaters of the flesh," the boy said.

"In our history," the storyteller said, "they were the first

eaters of flesh. Many descendants have fallen from that lot, but their time as a people is almost up."

"How do you know?"

"I've walked these mountains for over sixty years now. I was not young when I began. I am an old man indeed. I watched them gather into a tribe larger than you can imagine. I watched their destruction. And over the years, we run into groups of the others less and less. Each group is smaller than the one before it. By the time you are my age, those others will be gone from the world."

"And only our people will be left?"

"In this world my son. In this world. But there are others. Worlds we will never reach. Worlds that go on apart from ours. Worlds that have forgotten our very existence in this wilderness we call home."

"The machine people? They are of these other worlds?"

"Across an ocean too vast for your simple mind to fathom. Across that ocean are the people that built the machines."

The boy nods his head. "I've always wanted to. I've always wanted to see the machines up close."

"And you know," the storyteller asked, "why it is forbidden?"

"Yes," the boy said abashed, "of course. I would never do it. But I've always been curious."

"So you know then, the story of farmers and cannibals.

Cain and Abel is the name that some call it."

"Yes, I know we must always stay away."

"Maybe one day, I'll tell you that story too. But for now we must rest."

The old man led the boy back towards the camp each enjoying the silence of the other.

CHAPTER VIII

The sun was bright in the morning but the camp had taken on a gloomy atmosphere. In the night a desperate attack had occurred. Three men armed with clubs stormed up the hillside onto the flat ground of the encampment. The men on watch sounded the alarm and in moments the camp was awakened.

Two of the assailants were dispatched immediately. The third was impaled but not before his club made contact with the head of one of the watchmen.

The watchman was not killed but he was concussed badly. He could not see straight and he could not stand up. He was laid on a blanket in the center of the camp. Every so often he vomited next to the blanket.

He was put under the care of the women who fetched him water and massaged his feet and legs.

It appeared at first that he might die. However, later in the day he was able to stand up. He still had difficulty walking but his dizziness was almost gone.

That night he was still nauseous but he could walk and joke with the other men of the camp. Another big catfish was caught that afternoon, and that evening there was much to celebrate. The clubbed man sat in the center and was served by each member of the group.

The boy delighted in handing the man a piece of fish. He delighted in bringing the water cup to the man's lips.

When the festivities were over, the storyteller put his arm around the boy and said, "You see. We will outlast them. Our ways, our stories, that's what makes us better. This is our last night in this encampment my boy. Tomorrow, we begin the climb."

With this said, the storyteller continued his tale.

Abraham spent the rest of the day by the side of his wife and child. The time was not wasted. Over and over Abraham rehearsed his plan for a late night escape. He did this mentally first. Sarah watched as he sat in the corner of the room with his lips moving. Then he shared the plan with Sarah and Iniko.

The plan was simple enough. Get to the basement without waking anyone. It was the contingencies that added complexity. For each contingency there was another plan. And each contingency was spoken and repeated until everyone remembered.

Almost everything that was needed for the rest of the journey was in the basement. And the basement could be reached easily enough. The problem was in the fact that the water bottles were still packed. The water bottles were packed but empty, and there was no running water in the basement.

Abraham was about to walk down to the basement to retrieve and fill the bottles when he heard the crack of the cellar door. The kings had arrived back home.

If he had filled the bottles then, the escape from the house would have been much easier. But Abraham was not hard on himself. There would not have been time, and if he had gotten caught in the act his situation would have been very grave indeed.

Later in the afternoon, Abraham took the jug that he had received the day before down to the water pump. The pump was in the downstairs bathroom. Neither the faucet nor the toilet worked, but the jerry-rigged hand pump that stood in the middle of the floor could produce a jug full in no time at all.

Abraham put his hand on the lever with the jug held up to the spout and pulled down rhythmically. With each pull the lever squeaked loudly. It squeaked loudly enough that it could be heard throughout the entire house.

Abraham shook his head. He shook his head and shifted his weight feeling the knife in his right cargo pocket. "I did not think I would have to," he mumbled to himself, "but to us they would do worse. I have no choice."

He turned around with the full jug in his hand and was greeted unexpectedly by Zoar.

"Squeaky pump," Zoar said and nothing else.

"Yes it is," Abraham replied uncomfortably, "did you rig it yourselves?"

"Was here when we took the place," Zoar answered. "The farmer who owned it, seemed like a useful fella. No, we couldn't of rigged nothing so fancy as that. Just hope it never fails. There ain't no water to get otherwise. Reservoir is poison."

"How do you know? How do you know if none of you ever tried it?"

Zoar directed his laughter towards himself. "No-one said that," he replied. "No, one of us here tried it. He ain't been right since."

"Bera?" Abraham questioned.

"Before he took the water," Zoar answered, "he was normal as you or me. He drank just a little bit. Went crazy. We had another fella back then too. He drank a good bit more. He was crazed for an hour or so. Crazy as all hell. Went at Shem with a knife. Gave him that nick on the noggin. Knife went right through the skull. Into the brain a little bit. He pulled the knife out and went after Shinab. That's when Birsha shot him."

"So, the water doesn't kill exactly," Abraham said. "People who drink it go crazy?"

"That seems about right," Zoar answered.

Abraham went up to the bedroom and retold his
conversation with Zoar to his wife Sarah.

"I cannot believe it," was her response. "No, I cannot."

Abraham knew what she was thinking. "Yes, it must be the
same," he said.

"It's just like the report we heard on the radio," Sarah said.
"That is what happened in the city. The people were forced
to report to the registration centers. Shortly after, the entire
city was anarchy. The people had gone mad. This is not a
coincidence."

"Maybe they tried the poison out here first," Abraham said.

Sarah nodded her head and retreated into her thoughts.

Iniko had been listening from the mattress on the other side
of the bedroom. He seemed miserable. His knees were
tucked into his chest. His arms were around his knees. His
head was down. He appeared miserable but he was happy
that his parents had taken him out of the city.

"My friends," Iniko said suddenly, "they're all gone."

Sarah turned her head towards her son. Comforting words
were on her lips, but before she could speak, Abraham
replied, "Yes son. Your friends are all dead."

Iniko did not cry. He lifted his head. His eyes were cold.

Sarah bit her lip and kept her distance. "Everyone we've

known," she said. "Our friends, our family, everyone is gone."

"Dead," Iniko said with his eyes staring at the wall next to the door.

For the rest of the afternoon, Abraham sat on the mattress leaning against the wall. Sarah's head rested on his lap. His gaze traveled from the face of his wife back to the brooding figure of his son. He could see nothing else. The walls were bare. The floor was empty. The color of the room was a colorless tan. A ceiling fan above was motionless and covered with dust. Nothing in the room moved. For Abraham, nothing outside of the room existed. With his left hand he felt the curvature of his wife's hips, the hips that had carried the weight of his only son. With his right hand he caressed the handle of his knife.

In the evening dinner was had. It was similar to the morning meal. Ears of fresh corn, and a mixture of fresh green beans with grilled tomatoes were served. It all smelled of smoke and the fat that had been burned onto the grates of the grill.

Abraham hid his disgust. He ate the corn knowing what had been on the same grill the night before.

Iniko and Sarah ate with relish.

Abraham watched as his son and wife ate hungrily, devouring kernels of corn, biting deeply into each ear.

The red juice from the tomatoes dripped down his son's chin. Iniko wiped it with his forearm.

Birsha reminded everyone a second time that meat would be on the menu the following night. Shem and Shinab chuckled, eyeing Sarah, eyeing Iniko, eyeing Abraham as they chewed. "A feast," he called it, "in honor of Abram, Eshcol, and little Aner."

"In honor," Shem said sarcastically. Shinab elbowed him in the ribs.

Sarah and Iniko were too busy with the ears of corn and the grilled tomatoes to notice. Abraham noticed, but he pretended that he did not. All the while, the image of the human head that rested in the corner of the kitchen remained in the back of his mind, the image that he planned to keep secret from his wife and child for the rest of his days.

Under the table Abraham gripped the handle of his knife. In a tone that was both pleasant and grateful, he said, "What hosts you are, to serve guests as you do."

Birsha smiled. Bera chortled. No-one noticed the turn of phrase.

The house was silent when Abraham ventured to poke his head out of the bedroom door into the hallway. He tiptoed over to the door of Birsha and Bera. Both were asleep. He went back to the bedroom. Iniko and Sarah were already awake. He had instructed them to get some sleep but neither was able to.

The family tiptoed down the hallway towards the stairs. At

the bottom of the stairs Abraham pivoted around the banister onto the steps that led down to the basement.

Sarah did this next.

Iniko tried to pivot around the banister just as his father had done but his foot slipped. Abraham was there to catch him. This was done without a sound.

In the basement, Abraham used the flashlight to retrieve the water bottles from the bag. The bottles were placed on the floor.

Next, Abraham unlocked the key to the padlock that was looped around the rail guns. He placed Iniko in a seated position across from the basement stairs. He gave Iniko a flashlight and a rail gun.

"Remember," Abraham whispered, "If it's anyone else, if it's anyone else, pull that trigger."

Abraham flipped the safety on the rail gun. "Don't think," he whispered, "pull the trigger."

Abraham took the knife and sheath out of his cargo pocket. He strapped the knife to his left leg. To his right leg, he secured one of the handguns that had been left on the floor of the basement.

Abraham took up half of the water bottles. Sarah took the other half.

Up the stairs Abraham and Sarah went. At the landing Abraham was careful to step over the board that had squeaked. Sarah stepped where Abraham stepped.

Together, they laid the bottles in the pump room. Abraham looked into Sarah's eyes. It was dark but he was able to find the whites. At the same moment, both Abraham and Sarah turned their heads towards the pump, the pump that squeaked, the pump that squeaked so loudly that it would wake the entire house.

With the bottles on the ground and the handle of the pump hanging still, Abraham pulled the knife from the sheath. Sarah drew her handgun.

Together they walked out of the pump room into the living room. The two bodies on the couches were snoring in unison. With the knife raised over his head, Abraham walked up to the nearest couch. The figure that lay there was belly up, breathing deeply, snoring loudly.

He raised the knife and followed the sound from the snoring to the exposed pig-like throat. The knife hung in the air for another moment when the loud blasts of automatic rifle fire filled the air.

Abraham fell suddenly to the floor. The two figures, which had been asleep on the couches, were up and in motion. Shem and Shinab rushed past Sarah without noticing her to the bedrooms upstairs.

Bursts of automatic rifle fire exploded through the windows of the house. Glass shattered, wood splintered, bullets crashed into the cushions of the couches.

Sarah rushed to Abraham. He was already sitting up.

"I'm alright!" he yelled. "Get down to the basement!"

At his heels, Sarah ran down to the basement. At the bottom of the steps they were greeted by the glare of a flashlight. The flashlight greeted them and nothing else.

Abraham ran to Iniko and took the rail gun. "Get the other gun," he yelled.

"Why don't we run for it?" Sarah shouted.

"Still need water. We can't leave without water."

"Whoever it is out there," Sarah replied, shouting over the blasts from the automatic rifles, "they want them, not us. Not our fight."

The firing could be heard from the upstairs of the house now too.

"If we go out there now," Abraham replied, "If we go now we're dead. They're not after us but if we go out there, they won't care who it is. Out there we're just targets trying to escape the house. It's too dark for them to tell who we are."

Sarah shook her head.

"If we fight them from here, we'll at least have cover."

Sarah nodded and picked up the rail gun.

Abraham ran up the steps. When he reached the top he crawled towards the furthest window on the ground floor. Sarah was right behind him. She stopped at the closer window. The firing was not directed towards the downstairs anymore. The five kings were upstairs. The attackers were firing at the upstairs windows.

Abraham extended the barrel of his rail gun out of the shattered window. He adjusted his scope. Through his scope he could see the heat of his enemies. It was dark, but he could see their heat.

Between the crosshairs of his scope, Abraham found the body of one of the attackers. He fired a single shot and the red body reeled backwards.

Abraham got down below the frame of the window. No firing came. He waited. Still no firing came.

He crawled over to Sarah. "They didn't see it was me. I got one but they didn't fire back."

"There's three others," Sarah said.

A moment later a crash could be heard from up above. "Damn you Chedorlaomer!" It was the voice of Birsha. "Damn you." Then the firing from above intensified.

"You'll be alright Zoar!" That was the voice of Shinab.

"Damn it. Damn it. Damn it. I'm hit. Damn it, I'm hit." That was again the voice of Shinab.

Abraham crawled back over to the far window. In his crosshairs he found a second body. He fired and the body reeled backwards.

A moment later Sarah did the same.

Suddenly the firing from upstairs ceased entirely. A choking, moaning sound could be heard. Then, a body crashed down the stairs slamming hard against the front door of the house.

Abraham was not watching the staircase when this
occurred. The final red body was between his crosshairs.
He pulled the trigger. The body reeled backwards.

"That's it," Sarah said. Using her scope she scanned the
front of the farm. "There were four."

"It was just like they said," Abraham replied, "Amraphel,
Arioch, Chedorlaomer, and the Tidal king. There were
four."

With the rail gun still in his hand, Abraham turned towards
the body that had fallen down the stairs.

"Slime pit…" the voice from the body said, "turned our
farm into a slime pit." It was Birsha. He was holding his
stomach. There was not much time, but much suffering left
for him. Abraham lifted his rail gun up to the man's head.
He was about to fire but reconsidered.

He stepped over Birsha and walked upstairs. He kept his
rail gun on his shoulder.

The bedroom in which he had passed the previous night
was riddled with bullet holes. Zoar lay in one corner. His
eyes were empty.

Shem was next to the far wall. He had a whole in his head.
Shinab was at his feet. He was holding his stomach. Bera
was not there.

Abraham crossed the threshold into the hallway. He
checked Zoar's room. It was empty. He checked Birsha's

room. It was empty.

"Where are you hiding," Abraham mumbled. He walked down the stairs to find that Birsha had expired in the interval. He heard the sharp squeak of the water pump.

Half of the bottles were already full when Abraham approached Sarah.

"I'll fill them," she said. "Check on Iniko."

Abraham walked down the basement stairs and found Iniko shivering in the corner against the wall. The revolver was in his hand, and his hand hung limp over his knee.

He did not acknowledge his father's presence as Abraham walked down the stairs. He sat shivering, lethargic.

Abraham crossed the room and pulled the revolver out of the limp hand of his son. With the palm of his hand, he grasped the boy's chin, his fingers curling up the right side of the face. He pulled the chin up and stared into the boy's eyes.

Iniko trembled.

"Where's mother?" he asked.

"Filling the bottles," Abraham said. "Everyone else is dead."

"Bera," the boy said. Abraham turned his head towards the opened cellar door.

"Bera," Iniko said, "he ran down the stairs. It was not you.

He was not mom. I fired the revolver."

Abraham picked the revolver up. A shell was missing from the cylinder.

"He screamed," Iniko said. He sounded as if he were choking. "He screamed the most terrible…"

Abraham put his hand on the boy's face. "You did the right thing. Bera, all of them, they were bad men. You had to. You had no choice. You did the right thing."

"He ran. He was screaming."

"It's ok. You had to. You did the right thing."

Iniko was still shivering when Abraham got him back up to his feet and led him upstairs to the pump room. Sarah had just finished the final bottle. She had a bottle in each hand. The other bottles were on the floor. Abraham took two. Iniko took two.

Upon returning to the basement, Abraham heard an odd moaning sound. He put the two bottles down on the bottom step and drew the pistol from the holster. There was no draft. Abraham walked into the center of the room and noticed that the cellar door was now closed. He pulled the flashlight out of his pocket. The narrow beam focused on a huddled mass that lay naked in the far corner of the basement. Its movements were barely perceptible. With each moan, with each breath, the back heaved slightly upwards.

The light was on the mass for only a moment, for when the

beam struck the eyes of Bera, he became suddenly wild. The long sinewy arms flailed about. He screamed into the ceiling and his voice echoed back.

He made no charge for the beam that held steady in his direction. He flailed in place, an object of irredeemable despair.

Abraham kept the beam focused. There was no wound on the body. Slowly, he walked up to the beast. Within an arm's reach, Abraham said, "Bera, Bera."

The animal could not hear and Abraham was unwilling to sooth him as his old master did. And suddenly, Bera was still. His eyes found those of Abraham. With his eyes he found Abraham's soul.

"Take it," Bera squealed, "take it, take it, take it!"

Abraham shook his head. "Not a shoelatchet. Except for the water from that pump, I will not take anything from this house. Through your despicable thievery, I will not be made rich."

Bera squealed, "Take it, take it, take it!"

Abraham turned his back.

Sarah and Iniko were at the bottom of the staircase. He called them over towards the packs. The water was loaded. Abraham hauled his pack up onto his shoulders. Sarah and Iniko did the same.

Bera was still squealing when the family climbed the cellar stairs out into the cool open air and the dark, starry sky.

That night the family camped on the other side of the low hill that stood beyond the farm. A light breeze blew the grasses surrounding the tent. Sarah and Iniko slept within.

Abraham was laid out full on the grass. He felt the breeze in his week-old beard. He thought he felt the radiation of the moon on his recently stifled skin. The moon, which had been just past full on the night of their departure from the city, was now, on this night, slightly greater than half.

Moments from sleep, Abraham breathed in deep. The open air filled his lungs. He exhaled and morning had come.

The storyteller began to cough. When the fit was over he cleared his throat and said. "Tomorrow morning we leave this camp. Tomorrow morning we climb to the place of meeting, we climb to Church Peak. For now we must rest. Abraham sleeps, I sleep."

CHAPTER IX

The storyteller's dreams on that night were filled with the bleakest terror. The visions came and went too quickly for the poor old man to comprehend. The feeling of intense and all-encompassing dread was without a face, without distinguishable characteristics. Raw horror was his all.

The camp awoke early that morning. The tarps were taken down. Bags were packed and strapped. It was still early when the first steps were taken up the steep slope of the mountain.

The boy walked behind the storyteller the entire day. When the walking was finished, camp was setup. A meal was had. A fire was built, and the boy found his place next to the storyteller. The story began early this evening. The men and women of the group were in good spirits. For many years, the mountains had been safe from the others. Everyone listened as the storyteller resumed his tale.

When morning came, Abraham woke to find that the tent

had already been disassembled. Sarah and Iniko were sitting in the grass drinking water and finishing meal bars.

Abraham sat up.

"So," Sarah said, "my lazy husband, he's finally awake."

Abraham turned his head to the east. The sun was already a quarter of the way towards its zenith.

"How long have you…" Abraham began.

"Not as long as you probably think," Sarah answered, "we slept in too."

Abraham walked over to the place where Sarah and Iniko were sitting and reached into the pack that lay between them. He pulled out a meal bar. He opened it and took a large bite. He took a second bite and the bar was gone. Dropping the wrapper he picked up the water bottle gulping greedily. He reached into the pack for a second bar. This one, he ate more slowly, taking a bite, a gulp of water, and then another bite.

He was half way through the second bar when he sat next to his wife.

"I had not noticed them when we were trapped in the house," Abraham said. He was pointing at a cluster of chickens that were pecking at the ground inside of a wire fence.

"Me neither," Sarah responded. A rooster, standing apart, crowed.

"I did not hear him once," Abraham said.

"That house," Sarah replied, "sounds couldn't penetrate."

Abraham nodded his head. Something within the wire fence caught his eye. It was pure white. From a distance the shape of the pure white object appeared unnatural.

Abraham pulled himself up and walked over to the chicken wire.

As he got closer, the object became clearer. It was small. There were five fingers. The bone of the hand was bleached by the sun. He shook his head and his gaze wandered over to the place where the chickens were feeding.

There was dried corn that had been scattered on the ground. That was not what the chickens were pecking at. In the center of five large hens, heads bobbing up and down, there lay a foot. It was human.

Abraham walked back to Sarah and Iniko. He said nothing.

"We saw it earlier this morning," Sarah said with indifference in her eyes. "It was right that those men were killed last night. It would have been right if you killed them yourself. It would not have been murder."

"They were bad men," Iniko said. "We were in danger."

"There was something about that house," Abraham replied. "I was looking, but I could not see it."

Abraham was right. There was something wrong with that house, but only to those who could see it from an objective distance. For those living within its walls, surrounded by a culture mutually contrived, not through intelligent forethought, but through the necessity of every moment; it all would have appeared normal. It was years later that Abraham realized this.

The family sat in the grass as the sun climbed higher in the sky. In the distance a strange sound hummed. Abraham put his right hand over his eyes and looked in the direction of the sound. At first he saw nothing, but suddenly he could see it.

It was in the air. It was one of the flying machines of the invaders.

"Grab the bags," Abraham said hurriedly.

There was a large chicken coup on the other side of the wire fence. Abraham ran for it holding the hand of Iniko. Sarah was only a footstep behind.

"Get on the other side of the coup," he said in a harsh whisper.

The machine was closer now.

Abraham turned the corner of the coup and slid down onto the ground. He pulled Iniko down with him. A moment later, Sarah was around the side of the coup. She fell hard landing on top of Abraham and Iniko.

The machine flew by. Abraham did not see it. His head was down. He heard it. It sounded like an eruption as it passed by the other side of the chicken coup.

For many moments no-one spoke.

Abraham picked his head up. The flying machine was out of sight.

Iniko trembled. "Was it coming for us," he whispered.

Sarah tousled his hair.

"Was it?" he asked again.

"Just for us?" Sarah said. "No, they wouldn't send it just for us."

Abraham shook his head and turned towards Sarah. "I don't think it's turning around. Maybe it was because of all the gunfire last night. It's just checking out the scene. Not much to see now."

Sarah and Iniko were still sitting.

"We should go," Abraham said. "We have remained here too long." He reached his hand down towards Sarah, who took it, standing up. Abraham picked Iniko up by the pack straps. "We will not see it again," he said looking into the eyes of his son.

Abraham turned around and walked towards the low hill. The farmhouse was beyond it; the road was beyond the farmhouse.

As the family passed the reservoir, Abraham's eyes were again mesmerized by the reflection in the pool. This time though it was different. He could not see the image of the low hill reflected in the glasslike water. Reflected in the glass was the farm house inverted. The image stood still and lifeless.

He could not see the depths of the reservoir, but he knew now of its dangers. The wavelike edges of the pool were covered in slime. The stench was awful. It was from the depths that the slime, that the stench, that the real nature of the pool originated. It showed only on the edges. The glasslike surface hid the massive expanse of its entirety, a cesspool of slime and stench.

Abraham tore his eyes away from the illusion of the surface and turned his vision to the road ahead.

The afternoon sun was hot. Abraham did not want to stop because of the late morning and the promise of cover underneath the trees ahead. The mountains were looming and Abraham intended on reaching the base by nightfall.

From the base of the mountains, he was sure that he would find safety. The trees grew tall and thick. There were places to hide. There was shade from the sun. There were streams with fresh water and fresh fish. He even knew of a few plants that were edible.

The base of the mountain was still a long way off. Abraham stared down the long straight road. Every now and then he would see an object ahead. From a distance with little to gauge relative size, it was impossible to know what the object was, its mass, or how far away it was.

Abraham saw the large branch of a tree. From a distance it

appeared to be a dog. Then it was car bumper, then a rabbit. Finally, it was a stick.

In the distance, objects swayed with the heat lifting from the black road. Ahead it was all in motion; it was all an illusion.

The day was almost over when Abraham heard something behind. He turned around. Sarah and Iniko had already stopped walking and were staring at the figure that appeared to be moving up from behind them.

It swayed with heat rising off of the blackness of the road.

The road was black. The hazy figure was black and from a distance it first walked like a dog, then a large cat, then a dog, and finally a man.

All the while it howled with its face turned up towards the sky, and Abraham knew who this was.

The figure must have noticed the apprehension of Abraham and his family. The legs stopped moving, but the body continued to sway.

Abraham lifted his rail gun.

"Abraham," Sarah said. "No, he's harmless."

"Father," Iniko stammered. He said nothing else.

The rail gun cracked.

The figure did not move.

"Abraham, no," Sarah said.

"Relax," he replied, "I shot over his head."

Sarah let out her breath.

"You won't shoot him," she said.

"Even a good dog can go rabid," Abraham replied. "Only if I have to."

Abraham turned around. The howling from the creature continued.

For the remainder of the evening, Abraham turned around only twice. The figure was always at the same distance. It did not dare to venture nearer.

As the sun began to set, Abraham and his family were within reach of the tall forest that lined the side of the mountain. In spite of the full day of physical exertion, Abraham pushed forward. Darkness fell, and the family of Abraham was under the cover of the trees.

Abraham pitched the tent as Sarah prepared the camp. Abraham spoke as he worked.

"Should have shot him," he said.

"Stop that," Sarah replied.

"What if he comes after us in the night?"

"You know he won't."

"He's insane."

"He's an invalid, a child. You were never scared of him

before."

"I should have shot him," Abraham said with less conviction in his voice.

"You're better than that. You know he's harmless."

"It would not have been right," Abraham conceded. "But I would have slept easier tonight if I had."

"No," Sarah said. "I don't think you would have."

Abraham finished setting up the tent. He set up a small hammock next to the tent and sat beside his son.

"He's out there," Iniko said pointing. "I could see him lay down in the grass."

Abraham stood up and walked over to the figure that was lying in the grass.

"Bera," Abraham said. "Come on Bera, you can sleep next to the tent."

Bera did not move.

"Come on Bera."

Bera stood up slowly, clumsily, his long limbs flailing about.

He began bobbing his head. "Salty, Salty," he said. He howled once and followed Abraham.

"He has nothing," Abraham whispered to Sarah who was sitting beside him on a rock. Bera was lying across from them panting tiredly. Every so often he howled, but his voice was hoarse now and a grimace of pain filled his features each time.

"Well," Sarah whispered, "we have extra meal bars. From what I hear, there is plenty of water at the base of the mountain. There is even more as we climb up. We can spare some."

Abraham grimaced. "You want to feed him too. Alright."

Sarah unwrapped a meal bar. She threw it down on the ground next to Bera.

He whimpered and smelled the bar. At first it seemed as if he was not sure what to do with it. A moment later it was in his hands and he had taken a bite. He smiled, chortled to himself, and finished the bar with a second bite.

That night Abraham slept fitfully. With every sound of the forest he awoke. The wind blew and rustled the leaves of the trees. A small mammal scampered across the forest floor. A tree branch fell somewhere in the distance. With each noise Abraham was called out of his dreams with the deep set impression that Bera was committing some evil.

With each awakening Abraham glanced over at the sleeping creature. He was not quite sleeping on his belly, and he was not quite curled into a ball. His head rested on a forearm. He was in the grass. His countenance held a peace that can only be seen in the lesser beasts.

Morning finally came and Abraham crawled out of his hammock. Sarah and Iniko were still in the tent. Bera was standing in the grass. He smiled when he saw that Abraham was awake and walked over to him. The shock of black hair on his head appeared to be raised somehow. His ears pointed upwards and his dark brown eyes shone brightly.

Abraham was not sure what to do. Bera was an arm's length away and smelled as if he had been rolling in mud, piss, and feces.

"Sit down," Abraham said.

Bera sat down obediently.

Abraham then busied himself with dissembling the hammock. While taking down the straps he noticed movement in the tent. A few moments later Sarah was out of the tent and pulling meal bars out of the pack. She threw one down next to Bera's feet. He ate greedily. She placed the other three on a rock next to a water bottle. As she did so, Iniko's head popped out from the tent.

"That's the best I've slept since we left," Iniko declared.

Sarah smiled and lovingly called him lazy.

"Help me out with the tent, lazy bones," Sarah said. Together, Sarah and Iniko unhooked the poles and rolled up the tent.

The morning chores were completed. Sarah sat down on a rock and Iniko sat with his back leaning against that same rock. Abraham sat beside his wife and Bera was still sitting obediently in the grass. Abraham was about to throw Bera a meal bar when Sarah said, "Don't, I threw him one already."

Abraham nodded his head and bit into the meal bar that
was in his hand.

The day's walk was the most strenuous yet. Many breaks
were taken as the family and Bera climbed the base of the
mountain. Late in the day, water was found. The bottles
were filled and all drank from the stream that poured out of
a gap in the mountain.

It was Abraham's idea to put down the packs and follow
the thin stream of water downhill. "There might be a pool
below," he said.

Abraham followed the stream as it curved around trees and
ducked under rocks. He followed and followed. Finally,
with Bera nipping at his heels, Abraham stopped short.
Bera nearly ran into him. Sarah and Iniko were only a few
steps behind.

Abraham stopped short at a shallow cliff from which the
stream dropped off a distance, which measured the height
of two men. At the bottom of the waterfall was a deep pool.
The water was running. The water was clean, clear, and
aqua blue.

Abraham, pouring sweat, found a way down. He tore off
his shoes, his pants, his shirt and jumped in. Sarah and
Iniko did the same.

With his hands Abraham scrubbed his entire body. The

week old sweat and grime felt as if it were peeling off his skin. Sarah and Iniko did the same.

All the while, Bera stood at the foot of the pool whining nervously. "Salty, Salty, Salty," he cried as the family of Abraham splashed each other in the pool.

"Salty, Salty," Bera cried getting louder, getting so loud that Abraham looked up in concern. A moment later, Sarah was out of the pool. Abraham watched the curves of her nude body. Still wet, she dressed, soaking her clothing.

Sarah found Bera's eyes. His eyes were hidden deep within the sockets as he whined nervously. "Bera," she said. "Bera, you should wash as we washed. It's ok."

"Salty," was his response.

"Take off your clothes." Sarah said.

Obediently, Bera removed his shirt. Beneath the shirt was a matted coat of black chest hair. He removed his pants and his shoes. Sarah took the clothing, pretending not to notice the stench and walked back to the pool. She soaked each item, and rang each piece of clothing out. She soaked the clothing and rang it out.

Sarah took Bera's shirt, his pants, his socks, and hung these from the branch of a tree. She then took Bera by the arm. He recoiled only slightly.

At this, Abraham pulled himself out of the pool. He walked over to Bera. He took Bera's other arm. Together they walked Bera to the shallowest part of the pool.

Bera whined and screamed, "Salty," but did not resist in any other way. His feet touched the edge of the pool and a tremor went through his body, but he did not resist. "Salty," he screamed.

Sarah and Abraham walked him all the way in. The water was chest high for Bera. Sarah imitated the motions of scrubbing on her arms. Bera began to scrub. Sarah imitated the motions of scrubbing other parts of the body. Bera scrubbed.

"We can camp here tonight," Abraham said to Sarah as they sat Bera down on the bank of the pool. He was shivering slightly. He had stopped whining and no words came from his mouth.

"I'll wash the clothes," Sarah said. "It will be warm tonight. We will be warm enough without them."

"Ok," Abraham replied. "I'll take Iniko and Bera to get the bags."

Sarah nodded as Abraham helped Bera back up to his feet. "Come with us to get the bags." Bera bobbed his head and followed obediently.

The clothes were hung when Abraham returned. The sun was just starting to set and a peaceful twilight fell over the grove. The sun did not penetrate the foliage, but a fire had been lit at the bank of the pool. The glow of the fire shimmered off the water and threw fantastical gleams of light on the trunks and branches of trees. The sound of the waterfall was pleasantly constant. The thin stream fell over the smooth rocks and folded tranquilly into the pool below.

The water was cold. It was clear. It was clean.

Bera was no longer afraid of the pool. He sat before it on his hands and knees. He brought his chin down into the water and drank in gulps.

Abraham filled the water bottles and allowed Iniko to drink directly from the filter as he pumped.

Meal bars were taken out. Food in hand, Abraham spoke to Sarah. "Two days more," he said consulting his map. "Two days and we are on top."

Sarah smiled. Her mouth was full. She lifted the water bottle that stood next to her, took a sip and replied, "I never thought we would actually make it. Not after the bridge, the deserters, the thieves, the house."

Abraham nodded his head.

"What's it going to be like?" Iniko asked.

Abraham yawned contentedly. He lifted his head back and gazed up at the stars. "Up there," he said, "we will be alone. No-one could have made it up that far. There will be stockpiles of canned food. I would bet that there are fruit trees up at the hotel. I think I remember that from when we visited. There were rows of fruit trees. They must have been for decoration, but I remember the trees distinctly."

"What I wouldn't give for something fresh," Sarah said.

"I remember the trees," Abraham replied. "There was a lake too. I remember it being stocked pretty well with fish. And wild game too. We won't always need to use the guns for protection. When we know it's safe for sure, we can use our rounds for hunting."

"Why wouldn't it be safe?" Iniko questioned.

"That's not what I meant son," Abraham answered. "No, I'm sure it's safe. We just want to be positive about it before we use up our rounds."

With this, Iniko's apprehensions appeared to drift away. The rest of the night he sat in quiet rapture fantasizing about his new life on top of Church Peak.

He slept that night in the tent with Sarah. Abraham slept in the hammock. Bera slept in the grass next to the pool. All slept easy.

In the morning when Abraham awoke, he saw that Bera was already up. Sarah's pack was next to him. From the hammock it appeared that the bag had been rummaged through. Abraham got up in a single motion and bounded towards Bera with his right armed raised. Only two steps away, his hand held high, and Abraham saw the reason for the rummaged bag. He arrested his hand, allowed it to fall limp to his side, and held the scold hanging on the end of his tongue.

In front of Bera, three places were set. A single meal bar was laid in each family member's place. A bottle of water stood in the middle. Bera twisted around. His arms swung loosely around his body. The arms came to rest and he smiled up towards Abraham, whose bearing was no longer threatening; rather, he seemed compassionately confused.

Bera swung back around. He sat up straight. Abraham had never seen him sit this way before. He did not bob up and down. He did not whine or howl or exclaim nonsensical words. He sat up straight, and he smiled.

Abraham sat beside him. The hair on his head was no longer matted. The smell was there, but it was not as sharp. It was not outright unpleasant.

Bera's teeth were white, much whiter than would be expected. The unusually large canines slid up and over the lower lip when his mouth was closed. But the mouth was not closed now. He smiled with a slight gap between his lower and upper teeth. He breathed excitedly through his mouth, panting rhythmically.

A moment later Iniko popped out of the tent.

"Good morning," Abraham said.

"Hey dad," Iniko replied smiling. He gave Bera a pat on the head and sat next to his father.

"Is everyone ready to eat?" Sarah asked as her head slid through the opening of the tent.

"Bera has it all laid out," Abraham answered noticing that Bera did not place a bar in front of himself. "Come, sit with us." Bera's grin grew.

Abraham reached over to the pack and pulled out another bar. He did not throw it on the ground in front of Bera. He handed it to him.

After the morning meal, bottles were filled, and the march

up the mountain continued.

The load was lighter for all. A strap was used to secure water bottles to Bera's shoulders. On the narrow trail Bera walked behind Iniko who talked mindlessly most of the day. The topics were diverse and varied. He spoke of his life before the journey. He told Bera about his friends, and school, and the games he played when he was younger. He talked of what life would be like when they reached Church Peak.

All the while, Bera listened. He understood very little. He remembered nothing. But all the while, he listened.

Camp that night was set up early. Abraham found neither a stream nor a pool, yet the night was spent in equal comfort and security as it was the night before.

Many from the group were still awake when the storyteller finished speaking his tale for the evening. In one movement he was up. "That is all for tonight my friends. Old men must sleep." He caught the eye of the boy and motioned subtly towards a thin path which led into the thick of the forest. After a moment the boy followed.

"What did you think this evening?" the storyteller asked the boy.

"I was happy they spared Bera," the boy answered. "Is that why we take in the homeless?"

"It is," the storyteller answered. "Under one condition. You see, Bera followed the customs of Abraham. From the first, he followed his ways. It is under that condition only

that we take in those in want."

"Bera needed them," the boy agreed.

"No, no, my son. Careful with the way you say it. He was in want of them."

"In want," the boy repeated.

CHAPTER X

That night the storyteller was greeted by no nightmare. He woke relieved.

The day's walk was strenuous. The group climbed straight up through the rocks. Most of the metal ladders that had once aided the traveler in the ascent were long gone. Those that remained offered more peril than assistance. Metal spikes that had once held the ladders fast against the rocks still protruded out into space. These still bore the weight of a traveler's hand or foot, the spikes having been driven deeply into the rock.

But one would notice that the grey of the steel has changed over time. After a hand grips, the red-brown dust coats the palm. Even these spikes will be gone one day. Other handholds will be found, or perhaps a circuitous route, but these spikes, these ladders will never be replaced.

The storyteller had clambered over the final precipice when he stopped to sit. He was alone. The boy was ahead, not far, just ahead with the rest who were undoubtedly setting up camp. The site was only a few kilometers distant. The storyteller from this place could hear the familiar roar of the waterfall. He could hear it but was still too far to see it. Camp was to be set up within view of the falls. The old man was alone. He sat on top of a boulder and looked out over the valley that ended abruptly below. The cliff face stared up towards him.

For a moment he felt dizzy. He arrested his attention away from the distant ground below his feet. He looked out into the vast nothingness that stretched out before his eyes. And suddenly, the wasteland of mechanized factory farms that covered the valley below disappeared and his vision went blank.

"Am I dreaming," the storyteller wondered. He wondered this but heard it said back to him out loud. By degrees, the blank space gradually regained some color. Wheat gold filled the storytellers daydream. He looked down. His body had rematerialized but it appeared much different. He was no longer old and gray. The skin was no longer the red-brown color of fired clay. The fairness of his youth had returned. The skin was pale but sunburned, it was sunburned but it was not hardened leather.

The storyteller glanced back up. He was standing in a field of grass. He turned around and was awed by the structure of a beautiful building. The façade was comprised entirely of glass. He turned back around and saw a peculiar green bench. He walked up to the bench and felt the composite material with his fingertips. His eyes traveled from the bench to the poured concrete slab below. He reached down and felt the concrete with his fingertips. It was hard and perfectly smooth.

A violent crash struck behind him. Suddenly, the storyteller was no longer looking down at the concrete. A window in the façade of the building had been smashed. Through the window walked a ram, except it was not quite a ram. The face was not of a ram at all. It was the boy from the nightmare. It had horns. It had a thick fleece. The four legs were carried by hooves and not feet, but the face was of the boy.

The storyteller wanted to run to him. He wanted to stop it, but he could not move. He looked to the sky. "Save him, my son, save my son." But the angels never came.

The ram took three steps and turned so that its side faced the storyteller. The fleece on that side was bright red and in the center a knife had struck deep. The blade was hidden; the handle was all that could be seen.

"This dagger found its place," the boy said in the voice of a ram. "But the second. The second can be prevented."

The storyteller felt a sharp pain in his bare feet. He looked down. The concrete that had been perfectly smooth was now rubble. His eyes stared out into the field that was beyond the bench. Thousands of dead, burned out trees remained where the golden fields of wheat had stood.

"Abraham," the boy-ram said, "Do this, and you are absolved of your sin."

The storyteller covered his eyes. When he removed his hand the vision was gone. Before him were the valley below and the sky above. He stood up resolutely and walked towards the camp.

The boy met the storyteller at the base of the camp and took the old man by the hand. "I have never before seen it," the boy said excitedly. "Beautiful, it is beautiful."

The storyteller walked with the boy to the top of the falls. The water roared at the source of the three great rivers over the precipice down over three-thousand feet to the rocks below.

Together, the boy and the old man found smooth rocks on which to sit. The sun was at their backs. The storyteller resumed his tale.

Nothing was unusual about the next morning. The afternoon was normal. Throughout the day Abraham walked with Sarah. Iniko walked with Bera.

It was all very ordinary and then a pack strap snapped on Abraham's bag. The family stopped as he fixed it. The fixing took longer than expected. The strap was too short to tie. He tried to tie it, but after a few steps the weight of the bag caused the knot to slip. This happened three times. Finally, after digging through his bag, Abraham found a cord of rope that could be used for lashing the pack back together.

It worked, but much of the day had been wasted.

When the family reached the metal ladders, there were still

ladders then, the sun was already falling in the sky.

Abraham had never before walked this trail. With the map that had been printed from the car many, many days previously, Abraham judged the distance to be shorter than it was in actuality. He could not have known that the ladders should only be attempted at first light.

So when the ladders were reached, Abraham did not think twice. He put one hand on a steel rung and pulled himself and all his weight up. The family followed.

As Abraham and his family climbed the face of the mountain, the sun gradually fell towards the west. But Abraham could not have known at any time until twilight, how far the sun had gone down. For the entire afternoon it had been on the opposite side of the cliff. Throughout the entire ascent, the family was in shade.

Twilight came and Abraham began to see his error. As the sky darkened, the rungs of the ladders became increasingly harder to find. Abraham was the first to lose his footing. Both hands were on the rungs of a ladder. His right foot slipped below him, and the left foot went with it. He held on but the side of his face smashed hard into the smooth rock of the mountain.

He let out a grunt of pain and nothing else. His worry, he kept to himself.

"I can't see anything," Sarah called from below.

"Well," Abraham called back, "we can't stop here."

So the family continued in the growing dark.

The moon had not yet risen. It was now a half-moon waning and would not be up until the middle of the night.

Back then, Abraham did not know enough about the walk to wait for the moon. He did not think to take a rest, to take a break and continue later when the ascent could be finished by lunar light.

So the family continued.

Abraham began to climb faster. He climbed a ladder and took the flashlight out of his pocket. He shined it down below.

He tried this twice until Sarah told him to stop. The light was blinding; it was not helpful.

So they continued and were nearly at the top when Abraham heard a dreadful cry from below. This was in a place where the rocky ledge was at its narrowest. A slip on the ladder here could throw a traveler off the side of the mountain.

Abraham heard the scream and dropped his pack. He pulled the strap of the rail gun over his head and threw the weapon on the ground. Then he heard another scream. Bera was whining a wailing down below. He seemed as if he was bearing some great weight.

Abraham shined the flashlight and was greeted horribly by his greatest fear. Bera was leaning over the side of the cliff. Below Bera was Iniko who was desperately holding onto the edge of a rock, his feet dangling in the void.

The rest happened quickly. All in a moment Sarah had her son by the arm. Her and Bera pulled together but the weight was too much.

Abraham scaled down the ladder with his knife in hand. He reached over Sarah who was pulling on her son despairingly, knowing that she could not pull the weight, knowing that she was only delaying the inevitable, knowing that he was already gone. Abraham reached over with the knife and cut the first pack strap. The entire weight of the pack shifted to Iniko's left side. On his left side he lost his grip and clung with one hand. Bera fell to his stomach still holding onto the boy's right shoulder.

"Drop it," Abraham screamed. With his left hand Iniko was still holding onto the bag. "Drop it, drop the bag, let it go!"

Iniko straightened out his left arm, and silently the bag fell.

With all his strength Iniko pulled his left arm up onto the rock. Both hands were on it now. He hung for a second and heard the crashing sound of the bag smashing against the rocks below.

Sarah had his right arm. Bera had the right shoulder. Abraham came around to the left side. He grabbed the right wrist and the right elbow. He pulled his son back up onto the ledge. He pulled him up and the family fell back onto the flat ground of the trail.

"I'm sorry," Iniko began to say. It was too dark to see but tears were rolling down his cheeks. "I'm sorry dad. I'm sorry about the bag. I lost the supplies."

Abraham embraced his son. "It's ok. It's ok." It was too dark to see, but a tear rolled down his cheek.

Sarah held her son and he felt the warm wetness of her face pressed against his.

Abraham leaned back and noticed that Bera was beside him. He clapped Bera on the shoulder and held his hand there. "Good boy," Abraham said and could see the white teeth in the darkness. He could hear the contented panting.

Abraham kept Iniko in front of him for the rest of the ascent. It was not much further until the family reached the top. At the top it was easier to use the flashlights. The family could hear the roar of the waterfall. They walked a little further and found the source of the three rivers.

This, the storyteller said, is where they camped.

In the morning Abraham woke first. He rolled over to find that Bera had slept next to him. Bera's mouth was open and the tip of his tongue hung out past his teeth. Drool dripped down his cheek. He breathed out and Abraham gagged.

The gag reflex caused Abraham to roll in the opposite direction. As he regained his composure, he was reminded that the tent had not been set up the night before. Sarah and Iniko were curled together into a mutual fetal position, the mother's body wrapped around that of the child.

Seated now, Abraham rubbed his eyes and saw the two bags that were still packed tight lying in the dirt where they had been dropped the night before. He brought the palm of his hand up to his chin and cracked his neck in both directions. He put his hands behind him. His fingers felt the cool ground. He twisted and listened to the bones crack in his back. He twisted in the other direction and indulged in the satisfying pops.

He stood up. The narrow river was only a few steps away. The falls were only a short walk. Abraham followed the river to the sound of water falling in the distance. The air was very cool, much cooler than it had been in the valley and next to the road. He crossed his arms over his chest.

Abraham had not noticed during the ascent when he had crossed over the tree line. On the top, the ground was barren. He walked on red boulders. Halfway to the falls he stopped for a moment and kicked a thick pile of dust with his boot. He kicked a second time exposing the bare rock.

That is how it was when Abraham found it. It was bare rock covered in a layer of dust with no vegetation. It was not dead. It had never lived. Cold rock, dust, nothing else, all was lifeless and always had been.

"This is what is left to us," Abraham mumbled.

The sound of the waterfall grew louder. There was movement in it but still no life.

Finally, at the cliff Abraham put one foot on the ledge of a boulder, a boulder that had rested at the edge of the mountain for eons longer than man's fleeting existence. With that foot planted he shifted his weight forward staring down over the precipice. Straight down he looked and watched as the water dropped unknowingly towards the hard rocks below, colliding, but not smashing, flowing around the smoothed edges, breaking apart momentarily only to rejoin in the pool at the bottom. From the pool the river flowed out into the valley. Abraham could see the place where its tributaries broke off. What difference did it make? Each led to the ocean. From the ocean come the storms. And the storms bring the same water back up onto the mountain so that it can fall down these rocks once again.

Abraham tore his vision away. The image had him dizzy. Taking a step back he found a boulder that he could sit on. The sky was not completely clear, but there was no fog. He could see patches of blue sky. The sun was hidden behind clouds. Behind him the moon was still in the sky. It was visible through a small break in the clouds. There was blue and in the center hung the moon. It was not there long. The clouds shifted and it was gone.

He sat and watched the morning grow grey. He was lost in thought when he heard footsteps. He turned around. Still beautiful, he thought to himself as he watched the thin, dark figure of his wife, hips swaying mildly, big lips smiling inwardly, bright eyes staring penetratingly.

"We have been awake for some time," Sarah said answering her husband's questioning glance. "I," she continued, "I was already awake when you started cracking all those bones of yours. Iniko was sleeping so I stayed still." She walked up to the edge of the cliff and stared down at the falls. "It is beautiful. It's only a shame that we never came out here before. Before all this."

She turned around and sat next to her husband. He was sitting with his knees tucked up nearly to his chest. His elbows were resting on his knees, and his hands were supporting the weight of his chin. She slipped her hand around his elbow and rested her head on his shoulder.

"Bera saved him," Sarah said.

"I know."

"We did not lose much." Sarah said. "Some ammunition, extra clothes, a water bottle. That was it. "

"I haven't thought about it. But that's good."

"This evening we will be out of food," Sarah said.

"I thought that was coming."

"Should we ration it?" Sarah questioned.

"Not this morning," Abraham answered. "No, not until this afternoon. We'll take breakfast late and split bars this evening. That will give us something for tomorrow morning."

"Ok" she answered.

Abraham pulled out the map. "Let's start early today and then eat," he said after looking it over. "No breaking camp today. That will save us some time. If we start early we could be there by tonight. We'll camp outside the hotel so we can approach at a distance in the morning. Then we will never have to worry about food again."

"Iniko is with Bera. He cannot hear what you are saying."

Abraham nodded conceding her point.

"Well," Abraham said. "Either way, we will never have to worry about it again. If it is as we have hoped, there will be enough to live on for years to come. If not. If there are others there, or if it's been looted, we have still done better than those who stayed in the city."

Sarah said nothing. She watched as Abraham stared into the narrow unconscious river. It flowed as one. From here on the boulder he was too far away to see over the precipice. He was too far away to watch the water fall unsuspectingly over the cliff, to collide with the rocks, to separate, and to reform into the lifeless pool below.

After the silence Sarah said, "What difference does it make?" She was looking out over the valley, the Vale of Siddim as it was called. From here she could just make out the ruined farm on which the family had stayed for three days and two nights. "Everything we have known. Everything is gone. The invaders came. Nothing could have prevented it. It was their will. How long can we live this way? What difference does it make?"

"We are alive," he answered. "And life allows for a narrow path."

Abraham stood up and pulled his wife up with him. She stood as a pillar. He kissed the place where a tear had rolled down her cheek. It tasted of salt.

When Abraham and Sarah returned to place where they had camped, Iniko and Bera were sitting by the river. Iniko splashed his feet. Bera chortled as droplets of water flew up towards his face. Iniko was laughing. He splashed again and Bera drew back with a large grin wrinkling his cheeks.

Abraham watched from a distance. He picked up his bag. Sarah picked up hers. The laughing from the river stopped. Bare feet ran over the smoothness of the boulders. Bera picked up the sling that carried the extra water. Iniko looked confusedly towards each parent. Sensing gravity, he sat next to his boots and pulled each over its foot.

"Are we going to eat first?" Iniko questioned.

Abraham hid his shame. "Soon. The distance today is long. But if we start now we will be at Church Peak this evening. We will walk until we are tired. We will eat. And then we will walk until we are there."

"We'll be there tonight! I didn't know we'd…" Iniko began excitedly, stopping himself as the stolid grimace on his father's face remained unchanged.

Sensing this, Abraham forced a smile. "Yes, tonight. We will be there tonight." He put a hand on his son's shoulder and showed the whites of his teeth, unable to hide the creeping darkness that had entered his crystal blue eyes.

Iniko did not see this. He was too filled with hope. Perhaps Bera noticed. For the first time in days, a small whine forced its way through his lips.

The walk that day was easy. The ups and downs of the plateau were mild; and besides, the weight had been redistributed. Bera and Iniko wore slings around their necks. A water bottle hung loosely on each side.

The path was wide. In many places the family was able to walk side by side.

The interior of the plateau held a diversity of vivid greens. The plant life was never taller than the waist of Abraham. There were no flowers. But the greens were richly varied and beautiful to look upon. As the day carried on, the sky above cleared. The clouds separated and there was more blue than gray.

At midday the family watched as the clouds cast long moving shadows on the low, wavy hills ahead. The path that day went in one direction; the shadows always moved towards the family, coming to meet them.

Each shadow could be seen from a long distance off. Each moved slowly, very slowly, yet each was inescapable, for each cloud moved in the direction the wind took it, and Abraham and his family were restricted to a singular narrow path.

Abraham felt the breeze on his face; he felt the moments reprieve from the sun's brightness when the shadow passed over. Both felt good, but only as a negation of an overexposure. If he was given a choice between the sun's brightness and could have only that, or the choice of permanent shade, he would undoubtedly take the former. He has no choice though. The shade will come when it comes. The sun shines when it shines.

He chose to walk forward with shadow approaching. If he turned around, the same shadows would overtake him. To meet darkness head on, or to turn his back and allow himself to be caught, that was the only choice he was free to make.

It was late in the morning when the family finally stopped. It was so late that the sun was nearly at the top of the sky. Abraham kept his pack on. He asked Sarah to turn around. From her pack he pulled out four meal bars. He kept one and gave out the other three. He opened the packaging and took a bite. Everyone was still standing. He reached over to one of the water bottles that hung loosely at Iniko's side. He took a heavy sip.

Bera imitated his master perfectly. He took a bite. He took a sip. Sarah shifted her weight from one foot to the other as she ate. Iniko stood as still as his father.

The meal was over and no-one had sat down. Abraham turned and began walking. His family followed.

As the sun began to set, Abraham took his first step up a long, relatively steep incline. This was the steepest incline of the day, and the space beyond the top was unknowable.

"We will find a place to camp on the bottom of this hill," Abraham said. "We have gone far enough today. We came up short but we covered a greater distance today than any day before."

No-one answered. The family was trudging along in a

single file now. No-one had spoken in a long time.

Abraham continued up the hill and could feel his muscles burning. Halfway and he turned around to see if his family was keeping up. Bera was not quite at his heals. Past Bera there was a long gap. Sarah was putting effort into each step. Her arms swung wide of her hips. Iniko was behind her holding onto the back of her pack. His face was red. His steps were wide but not long.

Abraham waited for his wife and son. "Iniko," he said. "Take my hand." Red-faced and breathing hard, Iniko took his father's hand.

"Almost there," he said.

As Abraham reached the top, with his son in hand, the slope of the hill waned. The ground was almost even when he was able to see over the hill at the slopes of other hills that stood in the distance. He took another step and could almost see into the shallow valley below. Another step and he could see a small lake in the furthest corner of the valley. Another step and he stopped walking entirely. He stopped and heard behind him the surprise of Bera, who was not expecting to stop so suddenly. Out in the center of the valley was an unnatural object that Abraham had not expected to see. Not yet at least, he had not expected to see it yet. He put his hand over his mouth.

Iniko could not see it. He was not as tall as his father. He let go of his father's hand and walked forward.

"It's here! That's it!"

Iniko, still red faced, jumped up and down. The bottles of water that were strung around the back of his neck bounced, colliding with his narrow abdomen.

"We're here! We made it!"

Bera responded to the enthusiasm with howls of pleasure.

Abraham stood still. His thumbs were wrapped tightly around his pack straps. His boots were planted in the earth below him. He rubbed the thick whiskers that had formed underneath his chin. A wry grin presented itself, but not of its own volition.

Sarah let her son embrace her. The bottles of water first struck her hips and upper thighs. His thin arms reached around her shoulders. The kiss that landed on her cheek was full of life, and it was wet.

"Come on," Iniko said turning back towards his father. "Let's go. We can make it tonight! Let's go."

Abraham stood unflinching. What stronger force exists for man than the exuberant persistence of the young? He felt his son's desire. It was right there. It was within reach, a short walk from here. But Abraham did not flinch.

"In the morning my son," Abraham replied. The grin had broadened condescendingly. "In the morning, Bera and I will go up alone. Precautions," he said, "we should be careful. I doubt to find anyone, but we must be careful. After all, we have met only one friend throughout our travels in this wilderness. We have met but one friend amongst the many that would have committed certain evil towards us if we had not acted preemptively."

Iniko staggered.

"Your father is right son," Sarah said. "It will be safer if we wait. What is one night when this is the place where we will spend the rest of our lives?"

"Ok," Iniko blurted. "I mean I was just excited. Of course, I mean you don't have to explain. I was just excited."

Abraham walked over and patted Iniko on the head.

"Take a look down below." Abraham pointed towards a cluster of rocks that seemed to have grown out of the side of the mountain. "Looks like a cave. Good place to camp."

Iniko nodded his head with reservation and the family walked down the hill towards the shallow cave. Whenever the shrubs surrounding the trail were low enough, Iniko turned his head towards the once abandoned hotel. He turned his head and kept it turned in that direction until the shrubs were once again too high for him to see it.

That night Abraham insisted that there be no fire. There was no argument. There was no question. Sarah nodded her head and set up the tent at the foot of the cave. The rations were distributed, and after eating, the family went to sleep. Sarah slept with an arm around Iniko. Bera slept in the cave. Abraham's thoughts raced all night as he lay on his back, his eyes pierced by the brightness of the stars, the skin on his cheeks chilled by the crisp mountaintop air. Half-crazed he lay unable to perceive the time he had left; the time he still had before morning when he would take the lonely walk down to the Church Peak Hotel. The stars were uncommonly bright in that night's heavy darkness. The moon came up late, a waning crescent.

When morning finally came, Abraham should have felt groggy. He had not slept at all. He had watched as the complete darkness of the night transformed into a cold eerie twilight. As the sun came up, the mountaintop was not filled with the sounds of birds. It was not that time of year. The sun came up with all its fervent brightness, yet the mountain was silent save for the occasional shifting of the sleepers, the arrhythmic breathing of Bera.

Abraham rose with the sun, nervous energy propelling him towards a seemingly unavoidable fate. He pulled on each of his boots and reached into the cave to awaken Bera. It took only a touch on the shoulder and Bera was up and out of the dwelling.

He heard shifting in the tent as he strapped a handgun on each thigh. On his belt, he wore the knife in its sheath.

"Be safe," Sarah whispered through the opening of the tent. Abraham took three steps and was at the foot of the tent. He bent over and kissed Sarah on the mouth. The rail gun was at the foot of the tent. He picked it up and slung it over his shoulder. Bera followed, as Abraham walked down the narrow path towards the Church Peak Hotel.

The path towards the hotel was rough, a footpath that had either fallen into a state of disuse, or had been recently made through the footsteps of wanders akin to Abraham.

The grass had either regrown in the places that a machine had once cut, or the path was newly formed the natural way.

As he walked, Abraham brushed the bottoms of his boots against the tops of large round rocks. He held his hand out to his side allowing the blades of grass to flow through the tips of his fingers. The grass grew straight up and in places it seemed as if it had been matted down. This was clear. The ground in front of Abraham was full of rocks, and the grass seemed as if it was trampled down.

Regardless, Abraham pressed on and Bera was a step behind always. The hotel grew larger in his vision. It was in the center of a wide overgrown field. These had all been the grounds once. At one time, and for many, many years the fields around the hotel had been manicured much like the fields of the machines. The grass was cut short though. It was cut no higher than the top of a man's foot. That was how it was when Abraham visited the hotel as a younger man. It was no longer that way; the grass stood even with his hips; the rich green was a lighter yellow-green.

The sun rose just above the hotel leaving the front of the building in shadow. The glass façade did not appear as a mirror, as it would if it were late in the day. Nevertheless it was impossible to see inside. Inside there was only shadow.

The sky was blue and the air was still. There was not a single cloud and on this rare day there was no fog. Everything was clear to Abraham and yet he walked on.

A small clearing came up on the right side of the footpath.

The grass here had been trampled down. In the center there was a circle formed with rocks. The circle was blackened but not smoking. Abraham paused a moment in this spot. He considered turning around. He did not. He turned away from the fire ring and continued down the narrow, beaten path.

Bera was quiet throughout the walk. He did not whine. He followed closely with his tongue hanging out the side of his mouth. Not once did Abraham turn around to see if his companion was following. It was unnecessary. Bera was not capable of perceiving the significance of the clearing, the trampled grass, the singular oasis in a wilderness of nothing.

As he approached, Abraham shouldered his rail gun. There were no obvious signs of occupancy on the outside of the building, but that was of no consequence. There had not been signs at the farmhouse either. Man in this wilderness, must fear his fellow creatures. The man who trusts, as Abraham found out over the course of the past week, does not survive long.

Abraham aimed the weapon towards the right side of the building. He aimed towards the left. Standing there with Bera beside him he felt like his feet had been planted in the ground. He shifted his weight but he could not take a step in the direction of the hotel.

Bera whined. He paced back and forth. He peered up towards Abraham in a state of anxious excitement.

"Alright," Abraham said. "Let's go boy." He took a step in

the direction of the hotel. He took a step and then another. The grand doors in the center of the glass façade were directly ahead. While he walked, Abraham looked continually to his right and then his left. He held the rail gun in front of him looking down the barrel with both eyes.

Abraham got closer and there was nothing left to look at on either side. The front of the building was concave. He was surrounded.

To see inside, Abraham was forced to put his rail gun down at his side. He cupped his hands over the glass and over his brow. It was dark. There were no obvious signs of dwellers.

He took a step back and turned around. He did not raise his rail gun. He left it at his side. Slouching slightly to his right, under the uneven weight of the gun, Abraham was momentarily struck by the presence of a large spider web. In front of him there was a railing. In the center of two posts, and hanging down from the rail, the sun struck the web candidly, displaying its perfection to its observer's eyes. The web was quite perfect. It filled the entire space. Anything flying in its path would surely be caught. If not for the sun, it would have been invisible.

Abraham examined the web carefully. He walked up to it and searched for the spider. He searched and he searched but the spider was not to be seen. 'Impossible' it seemed to Abraham. The creature who made this web would surely burn with pride. It would want to be seen next to the masterpiece. But alas, it was not to be seen. "Where could it hide?" Abraham wondered aloud. He stood up straight and was about to walk away when the fluttering of a moth brushed his cheek. He was startled for a moment but kept his eyes on the web. The moth fluttered for a second in front of his eyes and then the fluttering stopped. It was struggling now. The web had found its victim. The moth struggled violently and the web held tighter. "She'll have to show herself now," Abraham mumbled excitedly. But she did not. The creature struggled, but she did not show her face.

"Salty, salty," and Abraham awoke from the daydream. He turned around to find a bundle of nervousness. Bera had not been this way since the night at the pool. "Salty," he said again and began whining.

"Alright boy," Abraham answered. "Let's take a look inside."

Abraham walked up to the door; he pulled the handle towards him, and walked inside the hotel with his gun pointed towards the center of the reception room. The great room was dimly lit. There were chairs and tables, and many other objects that Abraham did not take note of. He crossed the room with Bera at his heels and headed towards the only hallway.

"Bera," Abraham whispered. "Check this door." Abraham stood with his rail gun aimed at the first door in the hallway. Ducking, Bera tried the handle. It was locked.

"Try that one," Abraham said.

The door on the other side of the hallway was locked as well. There were many doors on each side of the hallway. Abraham and Bera struggled with the handle of each door.

Every door was locked.

Abraham headed back towards the great room and Bera followed. The light increased as the pair walked up the hallway. They crossed the room to the furthest corner. This had been a place where food was prepared. Abraham remembered this place. He remembered dining here each night with his wife years and years ago. The same tables were in the same places. The counter had not changed.

Abraham walked behind the counter towards the door that led to the kitchen. This door had no handle. It had no lock. He pushed it forward and it opened.

The kitchen was small. There were a great many devices used for the preparation of meals. Abraham searched the room for food. He found nothing.

"Come on Bera," he said. "Come on, and help me find the door to the storage room."

Bera followed. In the right corner of the kitchen, Abraham spotted the handle of a door. He squinted towards Bera and said, "I'm not sure we will like what we find in here." He pulled the door handle towards him only the length of a finger and gasped at the smell.

Abraham closed the door quickly. "That was cold storage," he said.

He felt along the wall for another door handle. It was dark and he could not quite distinguish the outlines of the objects before him.

"What's this," Abraham said suddenly. "This has to be it."

He pulled the knob of the door towards his body. The door opened into a dark, deep closet. Abraham stuck his head in and could see that the room was at least four times the size of the kitchen. There were several rows of shelves standing in the middle of the room. There were shelves along each wall.

"Bera," Abraham exclaimed in sudden rapture, "this is it. This is all we'll ever need!"

He put his arm around the shoulders of Bera and exclaimed again, "This is all we need." Bera whined nervously until Abraham removed his arm.

Abraham allowed the rail gun to drop to his side. He reached over to one of the shelves and picked up the two closest cans. The cans were the same. Each had the label of 'Black Beans' printed in large black letters.

Neither of the men noticed upon exiting the kitchen that the top corner of the doorway was filled with the web of a great spider. In that web were the bodies of four helpless insects, two of which were still struggling. The spider was in hiding. It was waiting for these two.

Abraham and Bera retraced their steps back through the foyer of the hotel, out into the grass lined clearing surrounding the building, and onto the narrow path that led back to the cave.

They walked quickly and found upon arriving that Iniko and Sarah were waiting nervously, sitting on top of two large field stones. The tent was disassembled. The bags were packed.

"So," Sarah said standing up. Iniko did not move. He had been instructed not to.

Abraham approached without a smile. He put down the rail gun. Very seriously he said, "What do you think?"

Sarah slouched her shoulders. And then Abraham smiled. He pulled one of the cans out of his cargo pocket and tossed it to his wife. "So," he said smiling broadly now, "What do you think? Beans for breakfast?"

Sarah dropped the can and embraced her husband. She kissed his cheek. "I love you," she said. "I can't believe it. Is there enough for?"

"We will live here a long time before we run out," Abraham replied.

Iniko began to dance in ecstasy. "We made it! We made it!" he exclaimed. "It's so much bigger than our old home! Yes! Yes! Yes!" He continued in this way while Abraham and Sarah shared an intimate moment of relief, of unexpected salvation.

All the while Bera whined, Bera yelped nervously, Bera paced back and forth.

"Let's go now," Sarah said. "Let's just go. Breakfast can wait. We'll eat in our new home."

"Yea," Iniko agreed, "let's go. I'm not hungry yet anyway. I'm too excited to be hungry. Let's go dad, come on."

Abraham shook his head and continued to grin. "Alright," he said. "We should eat first, but alright. If that is what everyone wants."

"Last time," Sarah said as she picked up her pack. Iniko picked up his sling that held the water bottles. Bera picked up his.

"I'm not going to miss carrying this around," Iniko said.

Abraham picked his bag up.

He led the way through the narrow path that winds towards the Church Peak Hotel. His and his family's feet moved quickly towards a fate that had been determined in the very moment that Abraham conceived the idea of finding refuge in this seemingly abandoned building.

"We'll have this all to ourselves," Iniko proclaimed as the family approached the clearing.

Abraham and Sarah both were carrying rail guns. The weapons were pointed down at the ground.

"The door is right over here," Abraham said. His hand felt the railing as he walked up the steps. Iniko ran past his father. As he ran the bottles of water fell from his shoulders, but then he stopped abruptly. He nearly fell backwards. The door had swung open. The man standing behind it was wearing all black. His dark hair was slicked back.

The dark man took a step forward and the door swung closed behind him. He stood with his hands in his pockets.

The sharp point of his chin was accentuated with a thin black goatee. The brown skin of his face was otherwise cleanly shaven.

Abraham raised his rail gun.

"Welcome," the dark man said. "You have no need for that here my friends. Put the weapon down sir. If you just peer above my head, at the top of the building, you will find that my men could have shot you long ago. Phicol could have picked each of you off when you first arrived at the cave last night. But alas, what good would you be to us then."

All of this was said with an enchanting grin. The dark man stood back on his heels as he spoke. He stood unnervingly still. Only his lips moved, projecting an authoritative bass. He carried his shoulders high. He was not a tall man, and a natural slouch of the shoulders made him seem even less so.

"Allow me to introduce myself," the dark man said. "I am known here as Abimelech. My role here is that of an elected officer. I am not so bold as to call myself a leader. I am more of a spokesperson really. It is our Covenant that determines conduct here. But more of that later. Perhaps tomorrow morning, after you and your family have rested, we can discuss particulars. But for now, if you will, introduce me to your wife and child."

Abraham hesitated for a moment. He had been here before. "My sister actually," Abraham began but was interrupted.

"No man caresses, no man kisses his sister as passionately as we have observed you kiss and caress this woman. No, sir, she is not a sister. Perhaps a lover, but I would venture to guess not. This child did not come of thin air. No, he was born. His eyes are of his fathers. But his face. Everything of his face resembles that of the mother."

"You are mistaken," Abraham said simply.

"No, I doubt that I am. But have no fear. I have no desire to sleep with your wife, and I have no compulsion to murder you. Neither I nor any of the men here would condescend so low to do so. She is beautiful, but the Covenant that we live by forbids it strictly. Now, you are under no obligation to disclose the nature of your relationship with this woman because you have not yet agreed to the stipulations of the Covenant, but I do ask that you at least impart to me her given name."

"Sarah is the name of my wife," Abraham answered. "I am Abraham. This is my son Iniko. Bera, who is standing behind me, is of no blood relation. Through our travels, our paths crossed. He is a part of my family now."

"Very good," Abimelech answered. "I thank you for your honesty. It is a pleasure to meet all of you. And welcome to the Covenant of Church Peak."

Abraham nodded his head gravely.

"I would ask that you leave your firearms right there. And that knife that you are wearing at your side. Leave that too." He turned around moving only his shoulders. Abimelech's head remained stationary. "Michael, Gabriel," he called. Two angelic adolescents hurried quickly out of the door that was behind Abimelech. Help Abraham and

Sarah with their bags. Fifth room on the right. Let them in. That is where they will be staying."

Abraham dropped his rail gun. He unstrapped his sidearm. He unfastened his belt and pulled off the sheath of his knife. He dropped this on the ground, blade and all.

The boys led the family through the hotel. For Abraham, it felt as if he were being led towards an execution.

"Abimelech says you're stayin here," one of the boys said. Abraham could not tell which one it was. Michael was his guess. The other boy had not followed them in. The boy made no motion to unlock the door. To unlock the door, one would need to swipe a special type of card. For this, the building would have needed power, and the power had been cut off long before this day.

Abraham stood with his hands in the pockets of his hiking pants. He leaned back and thought for a moment that this may be a stay of execution. Suddenly, the door of the room swung open. The other boy was standing behind it.

"From inside's, only way to open em's," the boy said. "Well, come on in. Watcha waitin fer."

Abraham led the way into the room. His family followed.

"Make yerselfs at home," one of the boys said. Abraham did not turn around to see which one it was. "This be where you's be stayin'. This you're home naw. Welcome da covnant."

The door closed.

"I'm sorry," Abraham said to his family. "I…" He was unable to say anything else. He stood in the center of the lavishly decorated room.

Iniko knew better than to say anything.

After a few moments Sarah spoke. "I do not see it. These people, I don't think they mean us any harm. I see that you are disappointed. I know that you wanted to find this place abandoned. But these people are different from those that we met along the road. These appear to be decent people. Look at this place. Look at this room. How can you call this a failure?"

"How can you know for sure?" Abraham said sharply. There was fire in his eyes.

"Have faith," Sarah replied. "For this entire journey, I have had faith in you. From the first morning when you called me, when you told me to come to you instead of checking in at the registration center, I have had faith. If I had not had faith, I would be dead already. I would be in the city with all the other dead people. We have made it this far because of faith."

A bitter laugh escaped the lips of Abraham. "Foolish," he said. "Faith, you attribute our success to faith? Your trust in me, yes. That is why you are still alive. You had trust in me. But it was never faith upon which I relied. If I had had faith, I never would have made that call. If I had had faith, I would have gone to the registration center myself. I would be with all those dead people in the city. I never believed them. I never believed them and that is why we made it this far. I trusted myself above all else. I relied on myself and no-one else."

Iniko began to cry as he listened, misunderstanding the words of his father. Bera stood to his right. He was not whining. He did not seem to feel any distress whatsoever.

Sarah stood thunderstruck. She did not know what to say. Abraham's logic was undeniable. She and her son had relied on every decision that her husband had made. Without doubt, she had contributed her share to the group. Abraham was making no claim against that. Iniko had done his part, and Bera had done his. But that was not the point. Abraham was not angry with anyone but himself.

"I think it will be ok," Sarah said beseechingly. "Really, Abraham, I think these are good people. He said they have rules. They have, what was it called, the Covenant? I think it will be ok."

Bitterly, Abraham reproached her, "If I know one thing, it is this; men speak most loudly when excited, and when planning a deception. And I do not take Abimelech to be an honest man."

"Then why would he have us stay here?"

"Why did Birsha welcome us into his home?" Abraham replied.

"He wanted us to fight for him." Sarah replied simply. "You know that."

Abraham shook his head angrily. "I was going to keep this

to myself but I suppose that I no longer can. That's not what they wanted. They were intending on eating us one at a time."

"That's insane," Sarah retorted. "No, Abraham that's insane."

"I looked into the kitchen," Abraham replied shaking his head. "I saw there the remains of a butchered corpse. That is what they fed us the first night. That is why there was no meat the next day."

"My God," Sarah said gagging. "My God."

"There is no god," Abraham replied. "Not in this world. Not for us. As food runs out that is what people resort to. That is what people have always resorted to. Some sooner than others."

"Not all people."

"No, of course not. But those that are willing to do anything to survive, even if it means murder; they have always existed. Birsha and the kings as they called themselves," Abraham said disgustedly, "They murdered the family that lived in the house before them. There was a limited supply of canned goods in the basement. I'll bet you that Birsha realized from the beginning that the food in the basement would have to be rationed. You saw it. There were crops in the back yard. There were a few chickens, but there was no guarantee that it would last. Those men weren't farmers. At the end of the season, after the crop had been taken in, what would they have done then? They couldn't have replanted. They would not have known how.

Travelers just like us, that was the staple of their diet. That's what those sick bastards lived off of."

"But these people," Sarah said. "I think they're…"

Abraham interrupted, "Yes, I acknowledge that they may be different. Yes, they might be. But it really doesn't make much of a difference now does it? We're under there power. We are completely disarmed. There are clearly a lot of them. They have controlled our every move since we spent our night at the cave. For the first time in over a week, our independence has been stripped; the power that we had over our actions has been taken; we can do nothing but have faith that these people will be different. This is no different than if we had stayed in the city, if we had went to the registration centers, if we had been poisoned with everyone else."

He sat down. The rich wooden chair was elegantly upholstered. He stared across the room towards the window that was covered in thick dark curtains. In front of the window was a large, deep-red, overstuffed couch.

Sarah said nothing. Iniko was crying and Bera stood solidly next to the boy.

A loud knock came at the door. No-one moved. Abraham shifted his weight in the chair and after a few moments, he stood up and answered the door.

A short, stout, dark man stood at the door holding a tray. In an uncommonly deep voice, deeper even than the voice of Abimelech, he said, "Greetings, I am sent from Abimelech. Your breakfast sir." He walked into the room and set the tray down on a small, ornate table. "Abimelech would like each of you to know that he understands your weariness. You must have been out in the wilderness for many nights, and he would like you to be his guests for today. You have no responsibilities aside from getting your rest, and joining the Covenant for the meal this evening. I will be up when it is time. Until then you are free to move about as you please."

"What if we decide to leave?" Abraham asked.

"You may do as you please," was his monotone response. "But I would not think it wise to leave with the provisions that you have. Save for this outpost, there are no sources of food in this area. It would be days before you found anything. Starvation would not be your demise though. These are savage lands. You know that as well as I do. Without defense, you would not last long in the wilderness."

"So our weapons, you refuse to give back our weapons?" Abraham asked cuttingly.

"That is not my decision. The Covenant strictly forbids against arming our potential enemies. If we were to give back your weapons, how could we trust that you would not use those weapons against us? Since the beginning of the Covenant, we have guarded the resources that this stronghold provides. To live here is both a blessing and a great responsibility. There are many who would see the Covenant overthrown. There are many who would murder for the food that is kept safe in our pantries."

"I see," Abraham replied.

"Well," the stout gentleman said, "if that is all, I will take my leave. Enjoy your breakfast. There are changes of the clothing in the closet. If you would like to bathe, the boys filled the tub with water this morning. I recommend that you do so. They left a few bottles of water in the bathroom as well. I look forward to seeing each of you this evening. I am sure that you will be much improved after having rested, bathed, and relaxed. Good day."

He walked out and shut the door.

Breakfast was eaten in silence. When Abraham finished eating, he walked over to the bed. He fell into a deep sleep.

The sky had darkened completely when the storyteller said, "I believe we missed the evening meal my son."

The boy, with his knees tucked up to his chest, nodded his head. "I did not want you to stop," he replied.

"Well, that is enough for tonight. Tomorrow night, tomorrow night we finish the tale. Let us go back to the camp to see if there is anything left."

The boy followed the storyteller back to the camp. Together they scrambled over the smooth boulders surrounding the falls. They ate leftover fish and the boy went to sleep. Abraham was not tired. He walked around the camp. From inside a tent, he overheard two men talking. He could not see through the material of the tent but he knew the voices.

The first said, "They offered bullets. They found old bullets but have nothing to shoot them from. He showed me. They will fit our old guns. All they want is two of the children from the camp."

The second replied, "That is all. A small price to pay. The hunt will be easy this season and for many seasons to come."

The first replied, "It will be easy. We will make it seem like they wandered off. Take the boy that's been following around Abram. The one he's been telling his story to. Take him; he will not be missed."

The second answered, "Yes, but who else..."

The storyteller did not stay to listen to anything else. The speakers in the tent were respected men. If he spoke against them, his word might be questioned.

He found his bag and pulled out an ancient leather sheath. The handle of a knife stuck out from the leather. The butt of the handle was in the shape of an octagon. Printed on the sheath were a word and a number: "Survival" "1976". He found where the boy was sleeping. He lied down with the knife grasped tightly in his hand.

CHAPTER XI

The morning came and the storyteller woke with a start. He had not dreamt. Two nights in a row he had slept without the nightmare. He feared that it would come to him again during the day.

The boy was still asleep by his side. The knife was still in the old man's hand.

This was the last day of the journey. By nightfall the group would be at the Ruins of Church Peak. They would be joined there by friends who they had not seen in a year. The end of the pilgrimage and the beginning of the celebration were only a day's walk away.

Yet the storyteller was changed in appearance and not for the better. He wore the knife on his belt and his eyes shifted suspiciously in his head.

"What's that for?" the boy asked pointing towards the knife.

The storyteller had no response prepared. He hesitated awkwardly for a moment and then finally said, "I... I have always worn it... for the last day that is. I wear it for Abraham. It reminds me of why we make this pilgrimage."

"Ok," the boy said seeing nothing but sincerity in the venerable traveler's response.

"That handle," the boy said. "For some reason it seems familiar."

"I..." the storyteller replied, "I have worn it before. It must have been when you first joined the group."

"I don't..." the boy did not finish his thought. He did not want to contradict the man that he respected above all others in the world.

"While we walk," the storyteller said. "I will tell the end of the story."

He said this and he began the conclusion of his tale.

Abraham woke to a foggy stupor. He had slept heavily, for he did not sleep the night before. He had dreamed of the horrible and of the grotesque. For the rest of his natural life Abraham would be haunted by the nightmare that came to him that afternoon. Upon waking though, he only remembered the dream in flashes, in dislocated images. He saw a heifer, a goat, and a young boy with a dagger wound from which black blood flowed. The soul escaped from the young boy's body. "Disinherited" it said. There was more but Abraham could not remember it. That was of no consequence. He was destined to see the complete vision soon enough.

Upon waking, Abraham was unable to move. He had that odd sensation that sometimes follows a deep sleep in the middle of the day. His mind had awoken, but his body would not move; it would not respond.

He could hear though. He could hear the whispering of Sarah and Iniko.

At last he could move. Abraham rolled over gently. He rolled over and the whispering did not stop.

"Don't worry about what he said," Sarah whispered to Iniko. "Your father is under a lot of stress. This is just like when you were younger. He is under a lot of stress and he is not thinking clearly. These are nice people. We found a nice home for ourselves."

"I know mom," Iniko replied whispering. "I was just scared when he was screaming at you like that. Everyone seems nice and there are other boys here too."

"Good," Sarah whispered. "When he wakes up you be respectful and agreeable. He'll see after tonight. He was just tired and under a lot of stress. He will be thinking more clearly when he wakes up."

Abraham turned back over. His movement was loud enough to garner the attention of his wife and child. The whispering stopped.

"He's awake," Sarah said mirthfully. "It is almost dark out. We were starting to get worried about you."

Abraham groaned and sat up in the bed.

The first object that he noticed was Bera who was lying down at the foot of the bed.

He turned towards Iniko. The boy seemed respectfully frightened.

"Come here boy," Abraham said.

Iniko walked over meekly.

"We are going to be alright," Abraham said. "You just do as I say. Stay close to me tonight. Stay close to your mother. Do not venture far from our reach. There are other boys, but you do not have to meet them yet. If we stay here, there will be plenty of time for that. Stay close until we know it is safe."

Iniko nodded.

"Maybe your mother is right," Abraham said. "Maybe she is right and these are not bad people. We have surely been in worse places. If something goes wrong, we will leave. We will find another place. That is what we have always done. That is what we will do."

Iniko nodded again.

"Fetch your father some water," Abraham instructed. Iniko walked towards the bathroom. "Sarah," Abraham said. "Have you had a chance to bathe?"

"All three of us have. Do you like my new outfit?"

Abraham studied her closely. She was in all black. Her long feminine figure, her dark tan skin smoldered in the dim light of late evening. Her long hair was down. He had not seen it that way since the day before the journey began. Her black locks fell in waves over the small curves of her breasts.

"I do," he said and nothing else. He looked on as Iniko brought him the bottle of water.

Abraham took two strong pulls on the bottle and put it down. "Maybe you are right," he said to Sarah. She walked over and kissed his forehead.

The great room with the large, two-story windows was the place where the people of the Covenant took their communal meals. A large circle in the center of the room was cleared. There were no chairs, no tables. The men and women, almost thirty of them, sat in a circle and chatted good-humoredly while the food was prepared outside over a fire.

When Abraham and his family arrived, they found that places within the circle had already been reserved for each of them. Iniko was expected to sit with the other children. Sarah was ushered over towards the small group of women. Abraham and Bera sat side by side with the men. On Abraham's right, was Abimelech.

"The place where you sit tonight," Abimelech intoned gravely, "is a place of great honor amongst the people of the Covenant. It is reserved for guests and men of recent achievement. When the meal arrives hot from the fire, it is you that it will be served to first. Each plate begins with the guest. Each plate ends its rotation with the elected officer."

Abraham eyed his host sharply. "I am honored."

"Tell me," Abimelech said, his features covered in shadow, "how is it that you came to be here. What path carried you into the fold of the Covenant?"

Abraham related his story without emotion. He spoke vaguely about the chain of circumstances that began in the city of Babel and terminated here at the top of Church Peak. He gave the places, the people, and the events without description.

At the end of this abridged account, Abraham sat motionless.

"A great many dangers you have seen and overcome," Abimelech said seriously. "It is a miracle that you survived. It is a miracle that you have made it this far. Have no fear. You and yours are safe now."

Abraham nodded his head. He did not thank his host.

"Tonight you dine as guests behind the protective arm of the Covenant. Tomorrow you decide if you will join us. Tomorrow you will know of our commandments. Tomorrow, in the morning, we will go up to the peak, for it is from the peak where the commandments are read."

"And what happens if we decide to leave?"

Earnestly, very earnestly Abimelech answered, "Everyone

is given a choice. We will not force you to join."

"I see."

"That is all for tomorrow," Abimelech repeated. "For tonight, hear of how the Covenant began. Hear of how our faith in the Great Power of the Sky, brought us to this solitary hilltop. Hear of how our faith provided for us the hidden manna of these great pantries in a time of distress and starvation. Hear of how faith and sacrifice brought the people of the Covenant together to live in this great oasis surrounded by nothing but ruins and wilderness."

As Abimelech spoke these words, his voice elevated to a pitch of religious fervor. The people of the Covenant who had been sitting and chatting stopped all at once to listen.

"People of the Covenant! Listen and observe as we are joined through my person by the Great Power in the Sky. It is He who wishes to speak tonight. It is He who will share our story."

Abimelech's face went through a series of distortions. The people of the Covenant sat in awed respect and fear. Abraham was visibly unaffected.

Abimelech stood up. His whole body shook. Wild contortions filled his frame.

At last, he was at peace. His eyes were rolled in the back of his head. He spoke now with an unnaturally deepened voice.

"Before the Covenant the people were those that worked

the land. The people were those that made the land fruitful. But the land was taken, the people dispossessed.

"Many thousands walked blindly in this wilderness of despair. The people walked and the people walked but without hope of salvation. All but the chosen fell and became the dust of the Earth.

"The chosen found each other at the base of the high mountain. The people were starved. The people had not eaten in over a moon's time. But the people climbed.

"There was thunder and there was lighting. The rain fell not from above but from behind. The wind pushed the people forward.

"And then the miracle was seen. The great bolt flashed bright, thrown down by the Great Power in the Sky. And that was the place of salvation. That was the steeple of Church Peak.

"The chosen gave cheer and the youngest of the party ran forth. He ran to the great bolt that was thrown from up high. He ran and a second bolt was thrown. The bolt crashed and the boy was gone.

"The chosen were filled with fear. The chosen stood unmoving and Abimelech said unto them 'Move thy feet. The boy is thy sacrifice. For the sacrifice of the boy, our safety is vouchsafed.'

"The feet of the chosen were driven forward. The chosen walked en masse. No-one ran alone."

As the final words escaped the mouth of Abimelech, he collapsed to the floor of the great room. The people kept their distance. Their fear, bolstered in that moment of great distress described in the speech of Abimelech, was as strong this evening as it was the night that the boy was struck by lightning. The people remained silent until it seemed as if Abimelech had regained his senses, until it appeared to them that the Great Power was gone.

Abraham glanced across the circle towards Sarah. There was fear in his eyes. He was not fearful of the Great Power that was described in the story; his fear was of the people who believed in it.

"You now see," Abimelech said to Abraham peering through the slits of his snakelike eyes, "the power of the Covenant. We were on the very point of destruction when we were saved. When the Great Power destroys the rest of this world, when he flings the rest of the world into the wilderness as he has done for us, it is we that will survive. It is we that will proliferate the species. From your story I can see his works. He has rained fire on the people of the city. It is only a matter of time before the rest of this world feels his wrath. Tomorrow, when you are given the opportunity Abraham, you and your family should join us. Join the chosen and inherit everything this world has to offer."

Abraham stared directly into the eyes of the serpent. "I will convince them."

The meal was then served. A woman holding a giant platter came up from behind Abraham. She handed him the platter.

"Use your hands. That is the tradition, "she said.

Abraham scooped beans into his right hand and brought the food up to his mouth.

"Now pass it to your right," the woman said.

Abraham passed the platter to Bera.

Several dishes were served this way. Each dish was passed around the circle until it reached Abimelech who ate the remains. There were several handfuls of food left when each platter reached him.

When the meal ended the people of the Covenant chatted quietly and retired to separate rooms for the night.

Back at the room Sarah asked Abraham to talk to her in the bathroom. She shut the door. In a whisper she said, "He's fucking crazy. He's fucking nuts. They're all fucking nuts."

Abraham nodded his head. "I don't think he's crazy."

"What?" Sarah asked in a harsh whisper, "you believe that shit?"

"No, no of course not," Abraham answered. "But he does not believe it either. He does it all to control them. The people here are crazy. They are crazy for believing him. But he is not. It is all an act. He knows what he is doing."

"We have to leave." Sarah said. "We'll steal enough food for the next few days and we will leave."

"I'm starting to think that we don't have to. Why not just play along," Abraham said. "It could not hurt us to play along. It is safe here. There is plenty of food. We could just play along."

Sarah considered for a moment. "I guess I didn't think of it that way. You don't think they would harm us, do you?"

"There seem to be fairly strict rules. The people here follow the rules out of fear. Did you see how fearful they were?"

"I did," Sarah replied sarcastically, "afraid of the Great Power... what the fuck?"

Abraham chuckled. "It works. That is why he does it. It keeps them in line. I didn't want to give up any power when we first arrived. I didn't want to give up my gun. But here, I don't think I need it anymore. I think we are safe here. I think what he is doing. I think it is good."

"Ok," Sarah replied. "I trust you."

Husband and wife walked out of the bathroom. Iniko and Bera had been playing a game next to the bed.

In the morning a knocking at the door woke Abraham and his family. Sarah opened the door. It was the stout gentleman.

"The morning meal will be served after the initiation ceremony," said the deep voice. "I will wait here as you dress. There is no need to bring anything besides yourselves."

"Ok," Sarah replied. Abraham was standing behind her. Bera and Iniko were playing a game beside the bed.

"Get dressed," Sarah said to Bera and Iniko. She and Abraham were already outfitted in the black clothes that they had found in the closet the night before.

Bera and Iniko pulled on pairs of black pants and the family was out the door following the stout figure down the long hallway towards the great room.

Outside, the sun was bright, but a solitary cloud was beginning to form in the near distance. Its shadow traversed slowly across the shallow, distant hills of the plateau. The cloud moved so gradually, and the change in relative position was so slight that no eye could perceive its progress. But it was moving in a single direction.

Abraham followed the short progression formed by the members of the Covenant. At its head was Abimelech. The line led towards a solitary hill. The hill was just above the Church Peak Hotel. At the top rested a single green bench. It was made of recycled plastic and was held in place by a slab of solid concrete. The bench faced inwards towards the hotel, towards the interior of the plateau. Behind the bench was a long gradual hill that fell down away from the plateau. The trees were thick.

At the top there was enough room for the people of the Covenant to stand in a large circle. Four of the men, Abraham did not know their names, held automatic rifles. Abimelech stood in the center, on top of the green, plastic bench.

"People of the Covenant," he exclaimed. "Last night we were joined by four new souls, four new potential brothers and sisters."

The people stood solemnly.

"Today, they will be given," he said, pausing dramatically, "the choice."

This was followed by low murmuring.

"Bring forth the holy implements," Abimelech commanded.

One of the men stepped forward. In his hands he carried two daggers.

Abraham stood perplexed, but no sign of concern showed.

"Now," Abimelech intoned, "before these initiates can join the ranks of the chosen, they must agree to the three commandments."

A low murmur followed.

"The first, there is one Great Power, there are no others, and that is thy god. The second, thou shalt not murder, steal, commit adultery, lie, or covet. The third, the head of each family must choose a member of his family to be sacrificed for the preservation of the Covenant."

Another low murmur followed. Abraham could see that the people of the Covenant were eyeing his son.

"Abraham," Abimelech exclaimed. "Who do you choose?"

"I…" Abraham replied. "I do not understand. What do you mean by sacrifice?"

"When the Great Power in the Sky showed to us the way to this oasis in the wilderness, he sacrificed a boy for our salvation. Every family that joins the Covenant must make the same sacrifice. It is in accordance with the third commandment."

"That," Abraham replied in growing disgust, "is insane. You cannot be serious."

At this, the people of the Covenant recoiled in terror. A woman could be heard shrieking, "He dares to speak against the Great Power!" But Abraham did not hear.

"You must choose," Abimelech said with a wave of his hand, silencing the Covenant. "It is customary to sacrifice the youngest. The most devout have always done so. But the Covenant allows a choice."

"This is insanity," Abraham proclaimed. His eyes searched the crowd. He found no support. "You have done this? You have all done this?"

"The Great Power chose for the first families. But everyone who has joined us, everyone has made the choice."

Abraham turned towards Sarah. She was holding the hand of her son. Bera stood next to Iniko. He wore the dumb expression of a lamb. When Bera noticed his masters gaze, he smiled. He would have wagged a tail if he had had one.

"We're leaving," Sarah said suddenly. "Abraham let's go!"

She grabbed his arm but he would not move.

"Let's go! These people are insane!"

Abraham did not move. All four automatic rifles were aimed at him and his family.

"Can we leave?" Abraham questioned. "Are we permitted to leave this place?"

"You could have left last night," Abimelech answered. "You could have left before you knew of the commandments. But you cannot leave now. No-one who has heard the commandments can leave."

Abraham met the eyes of his wife. He looked past her at Bera. Bera smiled.

"You must make the choice," Abimelech repeated.

"The choice…the choice…the choice…" was repeated by the people of the Covenant.

Abraham looked down at his son. He looked up at Bera.

He heard his wife say, "You have to." Tears were streaming down her cheeks.

"I will not kill my son," Abraham said trembling. "I cannot murder an innocent." Bera was still smiling.

The words, "I choose Bera," quivered out of Abraham's lips.

"The head has chosen… the head has chosen…" was repeated in monotones.

Abimelech handed Abraham a dagger. It was the same knife that Abraham had carried since the beginning of the journey.

"Seize him," Abimelech said pointing at Bera.

Cords were used to bind him. Bera whimpered. He whined. He shouted unintelligible monosyllables as he was laid at the feet of Abraham.

"The choice…the choice…"

"What am I to do?" Abraham asked. "How am I to satisfy this unnatural rite?"

"Just as the Great Power struck deep with the thunder bolt, drive the dagger deep into the man's heart!"

Abraham stood blankly with the dagger in his hand. The knuckles of his right hand whitened.

"Ahh," he bellowed. "I cannot."

One of the men carrying an automatic rifle stepped towards Abraham. The rifle was pointed at the center of Abraham's chest.

"This has happened before. Many men have grown weak in the moment of the choice. Take the boy!"

Three men grabbed Iniko. Sarah resisted them. One of the men struck her hard across the face. She fell to the ground.

"Don't," Abraham screamed. But he did not move. The rifle was pointed towards the center of his chest.

"The choice…the choice…"

Iniko was thrown down on the bench. Two cords were wrapped around his frame. One of the men held down his shoulders.

"The choice… the choice…"

"You must choose," Abimelech said with the other dagger in his hand. Drive the knife into the heart of that man, or it will be I that acts as the Great Power; it will be I that makes your sacrifice to the Covenant."

Abraham stood over the body of Bera. He was no longer wriggling. He stared up contentedly towards his master.

Abraham brought back the dagger. He held it high above his head. Bera smiled.

"How can I murder an innocent? This man has done no evil!"

"You must," Sarah shrieked. She was still on the ground, but now she was sitting up. Blood flowed thickly from her broken nose. "Do it Abraham. Do it!" She began to stand up but fell back on her butt. "Do it or I will!"

With effort she regained her feet. One of the men grabbed her from behind. He lifted her off her feet and slammed her back on the ground. He stayed on top of her. She could not move.

"It must be the head!" Abimelech exclaimed. "It can only be from the head!"

Sarah spoke no more. The fall had knocked her unconscious.

Abraham raised the knife again. He could hear the desperate crying of his son. He heard this and could not move. He was frozen with the knife in his hand, his knuckles white.

"The choice...the choice..."

Abraham knelt. He placed his left hand on Bera's right shoulder. He raised the knife high above his head.

"The choice... the choice..."

He watched as a single tear dropped from his eye and landed on the shoulder of Bera. His son was shrieking in fear. Bera smiled.

The knife began its descent. From up high above his head, the knife plunged downwards. But then, suddenly, it stopped. The tip hung in the air. It was a hands length away from the chest of Bera.

Abraham stood up. His knuckles were no longer white. He looked up towards the heavens, for salvation, for the archangel, but the angel never came. With all his breath he shouted, "I cannot murder this man in cold..."

Abraham's words suddenly ceased. A shriek and a grown silenced him. Abimelech had plunged his knife deep into the chest of Iniko. "NO!" Abraham screamed. "MY BOY!

NO!"

Abraham jumped over the body of Bera. He was grabbed by three men. He struggled but was hit hard in the head with the stock of an automatic rifle. He lay crumpled in an unconscious ball.

When Abraham woke up, Sarah tried to kill him. He did not resist. She was grabbed and restrained. Later that night she took her own life.

For nearly a week Abraham did not eat. He did not sleep. One of the women forced him to drink water. Bera sat by his side.

The week ended. On the seventh night Abraham packed his bag. When the Covenant was asleep, he stole food and water. He found his knife. He was not able to get into the locked room that held his guns. He felt some disappointment but nothing else. That same night, with Bera, he snuck out of the Church Peak Hotel to dwell alone in the wilderness, to wander endlessly through the forsaken lands of the discarded.

With the final words of the tale spoken, the old storyteller let out a deep sigh. "That is all," he said.

The boy nodded his head solemnly. "I wish it was not over," the boy said.

"You have brought a smile to an old man's face," the

storyteller replied. "Maybe someday I will tell it to you again, for someday I will be gone, and I would like my story to live on past my days in this world."

"You will tell it again," the boy said excitedly.

"Yes," the storyteller replied, "and again and again. And when I am gone, you will tell it."

The boy smiled, and as he did so, his eyes lifted. In the distance, beyond the hill, he could see for the first time: the Ruins of Church Peak.

CHAPTER XII

The boy walked with the storyteller down into the shallow valley. Together they passed a shallow cave. In front of the cave were three large boulders.

From the cave they walked on along the narrow trail. The boy could feel the tall grass that lined the trail with the fingers of each hand.

From this distance the ruins were clearly visible. Where the building once stood, there was a blackened crater. Plumes of smoke filled the air from several campfires. Men and women were scattered all over. Eleven of the twelve tribes were there. The final tribe, led by the storyteller and the boy, was only a short walk away.

The air was filled with shouts and revelry, and the boy walked gravely next to the old storyteller. Every so often the boy would look over curiously. Each time he noticed that the old man had his hand on the strange looking knife.

At the foot of the ruins, the storyteller was greeted merrily.

"Welcome back Abram!" a young man said. The old man replied with a toothy grin and nothing else.

This added to the boy's confusion. The old storyteller seemed to be a bit of a figure amongst these people. Within the group that the boy traveled with, the storyteller seemed to hold no special importance. But here, amongst the men and women of the other eleven tribes, he was treated as a distinguished guest.

A man from the boy's group nudged his shoulder. "He won't let us treat him that way," the man said. "He can't stop them from doing it."

The boy did not understand. "What do you mean?"

"He won't even let us call him by his real name," the man continued. "It draws too much attention' he says. 'Call me the storyteller' he says. He doesn't look it, but can you guess how old that man is?"

Astounded, the boy shrugged his shoulders.

"Late nineties is my guess," the man replied. "I wouldn't be surprised if he was over a hundred. Don't look it, but I'll tell you he is. If everything he says is true, he's been around since the beginning. He was already a man when the world ended."

"I don't understand," the boy said.

"Ask him," the man replied walking away. "Just ask him."

The figure of the man's body folded into the crowd.

The boy had lost sight of the storyteller and began to feel uncomfortable, for he had never been a part of such a large crowd. Squeezing behind the backs of four men of a different tribe, the boy withdrew and sighted a hill just beyond the ruins. On top of the hill he could see a solitary green bench.

The climb was brief. The boy extended his hand and felt the strange material of the bench. It was rough in texture. The recycled plastic was a material that he had never before felt. The boy looked down towards his feet. The concrete below the bench was nothing more than a pile of gravel.

He sat down. The bench faced towards the ruins. From this distance, he watched as the brothers and sisters of the tribes below reunited after a year's separation. As he sat, he watched a solitary cloud travel towards him from a distance.

The cloud was empty but it crept closer and the boy watched on. It was just above his head when he looked down.

It was the storyteller. The old man was walking quickly up the hill. There was distance in the old man's eyes, a glare that went above and beyond the boy's head. It was as if the old man were looking more than just past the boy. He appeared as if he were looking through space and back in time.

The boy was surprised when he saw the old man draw his knife. The storyteller gripped the handle and the boy could see the faint gleam of the blade.

Suddenly, the boy felt a hand around his neck. He was pulled backwards overtop the bench. The boy fought back. On the ground he struggled desperately against his abductors, but it was like the sheep fighting back against the wolf. He fought with all his might and then heard the firm, penetrating voice of the storyteller.

"Let the boy go."

One of the abductors stood up. His face was dark. He smelled of death.

"Why…what are you here for?" The abductor asked.

"Let go of that boy," the storyteller repeated.

"Abraham," the abductor snickered. "Don't you try to stop us. We've bargained for a good price."

"The life of another is not yours to give. You have no right to his life. Let the boy go, or you will forfeit the right to your own."

The abductor laughed condescendingly and returned to the work of securing the boy.

"As you wish," the old man said. He did not look to the sky. He looked down at the knife in his hand. The old man took three large steps towards the dark abductor. The man stood up and threw his fist at the face of the storyteller.

The blow was arrested by the hand of Abraham. He squeezed the wrist of the younger man and watched as the dark features twisted in pain. The abductor fell to his knees and Abraham drove the knife deep into his heart.

Abraham pulled the knife out.

The second abductor let go of the boy and was on his feet. Like a ram, he lunged at Abraham, tackling the old man, bringing him to the ground.

Abraham was on the ground, but the head of the younger man was underneath his left arm. The knife was still in his right. He turned the knife over and plunged it into the young man's back. The blade slipped between two ribs and stabbed into the young man's beating heart.

Abraham let go of the handle. He could feel that the man was dead.

He slid out from under the dead man, breathed out deeply, and stumbled over to the boy. He pulled the boy towards his chest and embraced him with tears in his eyes.

"No more shall I dream," the old man said. "Finally, I may rest."

The boy did not understand. He took a step back. His eyes were dry. "Why did he call you…"

Crying, Abraham answered "That is my name, my son. That is my name."

ABOUT THE AUTHOR

Eric James-Olson is the author of three novels and several short stories. *But the Angels Never Came* is a prequel to *Farmers and Cannibals*, his first published work. James-Olson has two sequels planned. The first, *Just After the Fall,* is written and slated for release in April 2014. The second, *Whom Cain Slew,* will be released in December 2015. In addition to writing, James-Olson is a high school English teacher and an outdoor enthusiast. He lives with his wife and daughter in the hills of West Virginia.

Made in the USA
Charleston, SC
21 September 2014